I0520201

Nothing Sacred

and other stories

by

RICHIE GOLDSTEIN

ISBN: 978-1-5323-9698-4

"The Middle East has a way of exposing the vanities of all foreign-policy thinkers."
—Steve Coll

"We were too late in discovering our species had been unknowingly charged with the stewardship of maintaining a precious equilibrium, and due to the absence of our collective wisdom, our remaining time is now beyond this natural world, where we are but subjects to the wrath of thermodynamics."
—Daniel A. Drumright

Neither of these two quotes have anything at all to do with the following stories. I include them, because to me, they are indisputably accurate. Good luck to all of us, though it'll undoubtedly take more than luck to weather the storm. Oh well.

Cover art by instantjubilation.com
Layout by Penny Panlener Graphics

Dedicated to Steve, Jeff, and Norda, my brilliant editors/proofreaders.

Author contact: alphaauthor77@aol

STORIES

Also by Richie Goldstein

TRAFFIC NORTH
Crime on the Alaska/Russia Border

NOTHING SACRED

and other stories

Nothing Sacred

A SCANT TWO HOURS after the mooning of the low flying drone that had been hovering all day over the posh Beverly Hills neighborhood, a score of FBI agents, crammed into half a dozen black SUVs, began a meticulous and amazingly well-coordinated round-up of the six young men caught on high resolution video flashing their butts to the sky.

In its initial coverage of this bizarre event, the press was puzzled: how could the agents have known *exactly* who the mooners were? The suspects had been well disguised: V-for-Vendetta masks, NY Yankee baseball caps covering Rasta wigs, faded blue jeans, Alice Cooper T-shirts, and Keds High Top sneakers.

The disguises, clever as they were, apparently did not slow down the feds for even a second. They drove directly to the homes of the six teenagers, showed their startled families arrest warrants, and then speedily cuffed, Mirandized, and whisked away the 'Lunar Six,' as the young men soon came to be known.

The quick apprehension of the ass flashers did not allay the public's aroused curiosity. The question remained: how did the FBI identify the offenders so quickly and with seemingly so little hard evidence?

The answer showed up a few days later in an on-line posting at Wire/Mate.com, an exceedingly obscure, for-nerds-only web site.

New Gluteus Recognition Software Used to Apprehend 'Lunar Six'

The Federal Bureau of Investigation announced today that it has developed rear-end identification software.

According to Special Agent Stepan Kasimierski of the FBI's Los Angeles Field Office, the new technology, called *ButtSolve*, was instrumental in identifying the 'Lunar Six' mooner-terrorists.

"This is better than fingerprints, and almost as sure-fire as DNA," said Kasimierski. "As you know, the swirls and patterns of the skin on our rear ends, as well as the angle of the anus are distinctly different for each of us. So, finding ID matches for the so-called 'Lunar Six' was easy. We had already collected their gluteus signatures from the toilets at Seaside High School, where all are currently students. Once the Homeland Security drone photographed their rear ends, those images were instantly relayed back to the FBI's new database, REAM-IT (Rear End/Anus Methodology and Information Taskforce). We had those little buggers ID-ed before they got home," the agent said with a chuckle.

The public, to say the least, was horrified by the revelation that its tushes were now open for the world to see, inspect, and identify!

Calls for Washington to do something and for the President to act thundered across the nation.

Congress (naturally) dithered. They divided themselves up along partisan lines, each side accusing the other of "being soft" on butt-terrorism.

When it was discovered, however, that the toilets in both the House and Senate chambers of Congress were transmitting legislative ass-scans to the REAM-IT database, things really started to get hot.

In a poorly thought-out effort to preserve the sanctity of their bottoms, our federal legislators insisted that Porta Potties be installed throughout the Capitol Building, including in the huge, marbled rotunda. Unfortunately, the excellent acoustics in that hallowed, high-domed chamber allowed passers-by to become more intimate with their representatives' bowel movements than anyone thought necessary.

A special Congressional *ad hoc* subcommittee was hastily convened to assess the legality of *ButtSolve*. Witnesses were called, among them the Attorney General.

Asked by what authority the previously unheard of technology came to be installed at Seaside High as well as in the nation's Capitol, the AG shrugged. "Both Bush's Patriot Act and Obama's National Defense Authorization Act give us all the authority we need to protect law abiding Americans. I really don't know what all the fuss is about," the AG said. "*ButtSolve* is everywhere. You can hardly use any public toilet across the country these days without having your rear end scanned," he added.

Hearing this revelation, the committee members reacted in righteous indignation. Shouts for a special prosecutor, for the AG's removal from office, and for former President Obama to finally confess his Kenyan birth spewed forth from the hysterical legislators.

But the country's chief law enforcement officer insisted that the technology was absolutely essential to American security. In an interview with Breitbart News, the AG cautioned the nation, "Folks, I'm not sure you are aware of this, but our country has an ass recognition gap with Beijing. If we allow the Chinese to perfect rear end identification before we do, there won't be a safe toilet in the industrial world. Then what?

Do we become bears? Do we start pooping in the woods? I think not, ladies and gentlemen."

Our congressmen and women seemed stunned by this latest ass-gap information and quieted down, somewhat.

The public's mood, however, remained volatile. And as upset as they were about their rear ends' availability for inspection, Americans now found their daily speech patterns also seriously compromised: *ass-whipping, ass wipe, whoop ass, kick your ass, butt-face, butt hole, kiss my ass, ass kisser, (put your head between your legs and) kiss your ass goodbye, tight ass, candy ass, dumb ass, smart ass, stick it up your ass, move your ass, get your ass in gear, fat ass, lard ass, jerk ass, bad ass, and asshole*—some of America's most beloved turns of speech—now had to be used with much greater circumspection since it was not known exactly whose rear ends might show up in the REAM-IT database. Retaliation took the form of vicious personal jokes as well as secretly placed Whoopee Cushions.

But if the government seemed unable to help, a can-do American public attempted to remedy the problem on its own.

At first, people imagined that using disposable, paper toilet seat covers might hide their ass prints.

The *ButtSolve* hardware developers were way ahead of the curve on that one. They had reduced the portion of the rear end to be scanned to the area immediately around the anus, which (believe it or not) happens to be the most easily identifiable part of one's bottom.

Americans' determination to preserve their ass-privacy spurred the business community to take measures: cotton Ass Masques proved barely effective (you can imagine why). But an imported, thick skin cream, *Apres Moi - Le Derriere,* worked like a charm (although there *were* reports of isolated cases of STSAAS—Spontaneous Toilet Seat Ass Adherence Syndrome).

Of course, thousands of people—men mostly—began eschewing toilets altogether and started relieving themselves in the great outdoors.

America's growing fascination *with* and hunger *for* information about this most extraordinary crime/police action was insatiable, and at the same time, mostly unrequited. The reason: the quick disappearance of the suspects into the federal penal system. *Incommunicado* doesn't begin to express the depth of the hole into which the feds had deposited the mooner-terrorists. Family members, ACLU lawyers, Congressmen—no one was able to pierce the veil of secrecy the FBI had thrown over the Lunar Six.

Finally, the pressure on his administration reaching a crescendo of negative publicity and outright threats from the lunatic fringes—right *and* left—the President instructed his Justice Department to comply with the *writ of habeas corpus* arranged by the defendants' lawyers.

So it was, on July 4, the six young men made their first, exceedingly brief, court appearance: a speedy arraignment, not guilty pleas entered on charges of urban terrorism, a quick denial of bail, and an even hastier remand back to their lock up in Guantanamo Bay.

A bemused international press could hardly contain itself. From Bengazi to Beijing, the world read about America's obsession with ass recognition. The French, recently stung by having to reconsider their own sexual history were especially delighted to heap scorn on their prissy cross-ocean allies. *"Les derrieres? Je m'en fou!"*

joked Marine le Pen.

As the American government prepared its case against the Lunar Six, speculation about the constitutionality of *ButtSolve* spilled out onto the pages of every newspaper in the land.

Legal experts defined the thorny dilemma: the Constitution's protections against an intrusive and overzealous state security apparatus were being weighed against the need to guard Americans from butt-terrorism.

Following a brief trial at which Abe Lloyd, champion of individual rights, matched lawyerly swords with John Mee, champion of legalized water boarding, the jury quickly found for the defendants and called for their immediate release.

The federal government, however, dug in its heels. Keeping the defendants under lock and key, the feds decided to take their case to the 9th Circuit Court of Appeals in San Francisco. That most liberal of federal courts unanimously upheld the lower court's finding of innocence and further declared *ButtSolve* to be "an unconstitutional intrusion into America's most private parts."

But the AG was not done. Not by a long shot. In a Fox News interview, he reiterated his commitment to the broadest possible use of *ButtSolve*. "We have a duty to preserve the Union," the AG told Fox. "And if that means sticking our noses into the public's toilets and up their rear ends, then so be it."

Accordingly, the 9th Circuit's decision was appealed, was quickly bumped up to the Supreme Court, and placed at the head of the docket for immediate hearing.

It seemed pretty clear that the conservative activists on the court, having no problem with ass-identification, would reverse the lower court's ruling, keep the defendants in prison, and allow the continued use of *ButtSolve.*

That is, until Wikileaks hacked into the REAM-IT database and threatened to release to the world a set of high res scans of the hirsute and gelatinous rear end of the court's newest member.

The next day, therefore, without comment, the Clerk of the Supreme Court announced that, by a 5-4 vote, *ButtSolve* had been ruled unconstitutional and the American people could return to their toilets free from the fear of public (or even pubic) exposure. A grateful nation breathed a collective sigh of relief.

Strangely, the FBI did not seem particularly upset by the Supremes' decision invalidating *ButtSolve.* Deep in the basement of the Hoover Building, our country's valiant defenders of the American Way are hard at work, spurred on by the pressing and continuing need for genital-ID vigilance.

According to an internal memo leaked recently to the New York Times, federal techies are currently working on two new programs. In anticipation of a serious pee-pee ID-gap with the renascent Russians, the feds are developing UMPIRE (Urine Mist Protocol Investigation and Research Enterprise); and in light of a looming turd info gap with the Developing World, the feds have created FECES (Federal Enforcement Control of Excretion Samples). The fact that a majority of the Developing World does not have access to public toilets has apparently not deterred the FBI's R & D teams.

And what of the Lunar Six?

The exonerated and erstwhile 'butt terrorists' were given a ticker-tape parade down Rodeo Drive in Beverly Hills. They told an adoring crowd that they are scheduled to appear this coming Friday night on Colbert, where they have promised to reprise the act that got them into trouble in the first place.

Tune in. Should be fun!

#

The Visitor

Elizabeth Ferragamo quickly climbs the stoop steps—two at a time—up to the Manhattan brownstone's small landing. *What's the rush?* she thinks. *I'm not even sure I want to be here.*

At the apartment house's vertical row of mailboxes, she checks the names until she finds *Dressler, Martina/ Jerome. 4C.*

For the past week, the thirty-five-year-old registered nurse has debated whether or not to visit her former teacher. She consulted with family and friends, found their opinions divided. She reminded them of his encouragement—years earlier—and how he so generously praised her work. They countered that his ultimate betrayal of her negates that past support.

When she finally decides a week ago that, yes, she'll come and meet with him—question him, demand to know 'why?'—she imagines how he'll react upon seeing her. In anticipation of the variety of his possible responses to her visit, she has prepared her own set of questions. She rehearses them, often speaking out loud

"Don't you remember that particular meeting?"

. . . in front of a mirror

"What do you have to say to me now, Jerry?"

. . . and arranging her features to reflect outrage, hurt, puzzlement

"What the hell were you thinking?"

Elizabeth hates the whole process, feels demeaned by it. She knows herself well, knows that confrontation is not her strong suit.

But here she is.

She pushes the Apartment 4C call button.

After a short wait, a woman's voice echoes tinnily through the intercom's mesh, "Yes, what is it?"

The reluctant visitor leans into the call box. "Hi. Mrs. Dressler? It's Elizabeth Ferragamo. I was a student in one of Jerry's workshops, four years ago. At the Y. The one on Sixty-third Street." Thinking these facts alone will gain her a door-buzzing admittance, Elizabeth pauses. But when there is a lengthening silence from the fourth floor, she rushes on, "I was in the neighborhood and thought I'd drop by. See Jerry. Say 'hi.'"

4C grants a tentative, "What was the name again?"

Elizabeth puts her mouth as close to the call box as she dares, repeats her name slowly, a syllable at a time.

The woman upstairs comes awake. "Oh, right. I remember your name now. Jerry spoke very highly of you. What is it you want?"

"Nothing much. Just wanted to say 'hello.' Jerry home?"

"No, he's not. He won't be back for an hour or so."

"Shoot. And I was hoping . . ." Elizabeth leaves it hanging. After a moment, she is rewarded.

"Well . . . would you like to come up? If you don't mind waiting. I could make some tea, or something."

"Great. That'd be great. Thanks."

A buzz and the visitor pushes open the massive front door and enters a small and dingy, poorly lit lobby. Four water-starved ferns hang in the foyer's glazed glass windows, effectively shutting out most of the light. The floor is a chipped, black and white tile parquet into which a well-worn path from the front door leads directly to the open elevator.

The lift makes a cranky ascent to the fourth floor and

when the door opens, a short, stout woman is waiting in front of Apartment 4C. She has thick, gray-streaked, dark hair that flows loosely around her shoulders and caresses a sweet and smiling round face. She is wearing jeans and flip-flops. A flower print apron covers a bright red blouse, sleeves rolled up to the elbows. Her plump, bare forearms are coated with a white dusting. She sees her visitor's questioning look. "Friday's bread day," she explains, wiping her hands on her apron. "I usually make several loaves for the week. Jerry goes through them pretty fast." She reaches to shake Elizabeth's hand. "Martina Dressler. I'm Jerry's wife. Please," she says, moving aside and inviting Elizabeth to enter.

The apartment is redolent with the aroma of baking bread, and something more—some kind of marinara, Elizabeth suspects.

"I'm making chicken alla puttanesca," Martina says. "It's Jerry's favorite. Kind of a celebration for us." She hesitates, then politely, if not enthusiastically, adds, "You're welcome to stay."

Elizabeth senses her hostess' lack of invitational enthusiasm. "Thanks, but I wouldn't want to presume . . ."

"OK, then. How 'bout some tea?"

"That would be nice."

"Be right back," Martina says and passes into the kitchen through a swinging door.

The visitor takes a seat at the round table in the center of the living room—there is no separate dining area. Her chair creaks, its green velvet upholstery shiny with age. The table is covered with a bare white cloth. The rest of the room is jammed with furniture that was new in the 1960s. There are a pair of immense and deeply indented armchairs that take up too much space. Three standing lamps—all leaning—guard low end tables. Covering the floor is a frayed, wine-colored carpet whose patterns have long ago been walked away. There is a radiator at each end of the room, and along the walls, crammed bookcases. French doors are open to a narrow balcony.

Martina returns, backing into the room through the swinging door. She carries plates, silverware, and a platter of antipasti—olives, feta, prosciutto, carrot sticks, and celery stalks. "While the tea's steeping, I thought we might have a nosh." She hands the visitor a plate, cream-colored, decorated with roses, and crazed with fine cracks. The edges are fluted and rimmed in gold.

"Lovely china," Elizabeth says.

"My grandmother's," Martina says, "same as the cutlery." She pushes the platter of antipasti towards her guest, gestures for her to take food, then seats herself.

Elizabeth is not hungry, has not come to eat. She has come for an accounting, an explanation, an apology. But to honor her hostess' attempt at hospitality, the guest takes a handful of olives, a small block of feta, and two pieces of the cured meat. "Celebrating?" she asks. "Anniversary? Birthday?"

"Neither," Martina says, her face wreathing into a wide smile. She squeezes her hands together in front of her chest as in prayerful thanks. "Jerry's signed with Random House. That's where he is right now." Martina closes her eyes, and then breathlessly, "They're going to publish a collection of his short stories. I can hardly *believe* it."

Elizabeth feels as if she's been punched in the stomach, can't catch her breath. She doesn't want to learn of Jerry's success, doesn't want to hear good news about him, yet can't help asking, "Random House? How . . .?" she trails off.

Martina takes her time, pausing for effect between sentences.

"He's been writing for thirty years.

Submitting his stories.

Getting rejected.

An occasional nibble.

An infrequent bite.

All those years I supported him.

Reference desk at the mid-town branch library.

For better or worse, right?"

Martina's tone turns sour. "We decided . . . early on we agreed *not* to have children. Couldn't afford them. But we lived with it. We lived for each other." She looks around her tiny apartment, laughs, "Thank god for rent control. We found this place twenty-nine years ago. Eight hundred a month then, only thirteen fifty now. The landlord's been trying for years to get us to move. Offered us five thousand dollars. I asked him, 'Where we gonna move we can afford? And with what crumby five grand are we supposed to buy a place?' But now, all that's changed."

Elizabeth is unnerved, too stunned to comment.

Martina hugs herself with happiness. She glows like a bride. "It all started with a wonderful short story Jerry wrote, *Crosstown Buses.* He submitted it to ten, twelve different writing competitions. Nothing. Until last year." Here, Martina sits back, triumphant. "Until *The Criterion* . . . you know the magazine?"

"Yes. I subscribe," Elizabeth is able to answer.

"They named it best short story of 2016. There was a thousand dollar prize. Nice. But *then* . . . out of the blue, Jerry gets a call from *The New Yorker*. From Mei Mei Chen, their literary editor. You've heard of her?"

"Yes. I've heard of her." Elizabeth sinks into her seat, lets her head tilt back, closes her eyes.

Martina doesn't register her guest's distressed body language. The author's wife is caught up in the tale of her family's unexpected good fortune. "*The New Yorker* bought Jerry's story. It'll be out in the November issue."

Elizabeth opens her eyes, looks up. She sees that a tracery of cobwebs has taken over an upper corner where the cracked plaster ceiling meets a cracked plaster wall. She wonders why the arachnids have been allowed to homestead.

"But there's more," Martina gushes.

Elizabeth thinks, *Christ! More? Like what? The Pulitzer? The Man Booker? Maybe the fucking Nobel Prize for Literature?* She leans forward and puts her elbows on the table, cups her face in her hands, fingers lacing over her forehead.

"Mei Mei Chen took the story to Random House. They go crazy for it." Martina pronounces 'crazy' as if it has half a dozen 'a's in it: *Craaaaaazy!* She pushes her chair back from the table and stands, lifted out of her seat, it appears, by some unseen force of elation.

"Random House asked to see Jerry's other stories. He took a week selecting them and settled on twenty-one. They picked ten. Ten," she repeats, a 'hooray' in her voice.

Just then, there are key sounds from the front door and Jerry yelling, "Marti, I'm home."

Another voice, Elizabeth thinks, *dripping with joy. Random House. Jesus Christ Almighty!*

Jerry strides in, smiling hugely at his wife. He is a

large man, flabby and balding. Elizabeth remembers him as disheveled, almost slovenly. But at this moment, he is jaunty, straight-backed, effervescent. Until he sees Elizabeth . . .

And his smile evaporates.

His mouth opens and closes like a bottom fish brought to the surface, gasping for air.

His back collapses into a slumping hump.

Elizabeth feels strangely discomfited—embarrassed by the reaction she has caused. She can't explain it. *I shouldn't have come,* she thinks. *I should have put the whole damn mess behind me.* And instead of one of the carefully barbed accusations she has rehearsed, she can only manage an apologetic, "Sorry for the surprise. I was nearby."

Martina notes her husband's shock at seeing the visitor. She looks at Elizabeth, wonderingly, suspiciously. She thinks perhaps there has been a past sexual liaison between her husband and his former student, but quickly dismisses the idea. She knows Jerry was a virgin when she met him and has hardly been out of her sight for their three decades together. But this scene—the three of them here in her living room, caught in this fraught tableau—seems to her to bristle with an electric and unknowable danger. She searches for a return to normalcy. Food, she thinks, food is the great normalizer. "Lunch is almost ready, sweetie," she says. "Chicken alla puttanesca."

Jerry remains rooted in place, slowly scans his living room, as though seeking an escape. He looks toward the apartment's open French doors.

Elizabeth follows his gaze. She hadn't noticed how detailed the doors are, beautifully latticed. She sees that beyond them, the balcony is a renovation in progress—a stepladder, tools, drop cloths.

"Jerry's building us some shelves and flower boxes," Martina says, too eagerly. "He's a wonderful carpenter."

The handyman shrugs, drags himself to the table, and drops into a seat. He takes a piece of celery from the platter, begins to gnaw on it absentmindedly.

"Jerr, dear. What is it?" Martina asks, worry clouding her voice. She walks to him and places a palm on his forehead, feeling for a fevered brow as an explanation for his sudden and obvious disquiet.

Jerry's lower lip trembles. He begins to whimper, as of someone awaiting a dawn execution who hears the gallows being tested in the adjacent courtyard. Tears pool in his eyes. He looks up at his wife, takes her palm, kisses it lovingly. "Elizabeth wrote *Crosstown Buses*. She read it to our class at the Y four years ago."

This pronouncement immobilizes Martina. A look of abject terror contorts her face as she realizes the implications of this news. Her shoulders begin to alternately hunch, then sag. They have acquired a life of their own, her body not knowing quite how to react. She stares at Elizabeth in disbelief. Almost inaudibly, "You wrote it?"

The author of *Crosstown Buses* hears the words *and* the inflection—not accusatory, but rather pleading, as if it were all a joke and Elizabeth will disavow Jerry's just-spoken confession and restore the luminous future that awaited the Dresslers, a future that Martina realizes has been irretrievably extinguished.

The deed fully exposed, literature's supreme crime laid bare and confessed to—why then, Elizabeth asks herself, does she feel drained, shrunken? Why is there no sense of victory?

She looks at Martina, standing there crushed, defeated. The guest wants to comfort her hostess, to soothe her anguish. Perhaps through a recounting of the details:

"It was the Wednesday before Thanksgiving. It was snowing like mad. I read the story to Jerry and to . . . Tony somebody. There were only three of us in class that night."

"Tony Carella," Jerry says, a handkerchief to his eyes. "Because of the weather, I didn't suppose . . . I didn't think anybody would show. But you did. And so did Tony. He came only to say goodbye. He had gotten a job abroad and this was his last workshop." Jerry turns to his wife, "Only he and I heard Elizabeth's story. And then *he* was gone." Jerry looks back at the author. "When I phoned you, months later, asking whether you had found a publisher and you said you hadn't and had actually stopped looking, I got the idea. But I didn't do anything right away, until last year . . ."

"When you sent it to *The Criterion*," the author finishes, softly. "Under your own name."

Jerry nods. "Best short story of the year, they said. Sent us a thousand bucks."

Martina is swaying and making small groaning sounds. She has laced her fingers together so tightly her knuckles are white. She hovers over her husband. "What have you done to me?" she whispers, an edge of venom in her voice.

Jerry ignores her, sees that he still holds the celery stalk. He raises it, contemplates a bite, but changes his mind, and lays it down on the tablecloth. He speaks into the air. "Then *The New Yorker* called. They wanted the story. Three thousand dollars. *The New Yorker*."

Elizabeth feels sapped of strength. She wants to disappear. She drops her head, focuses on the plate of food in front of her. She picks up her fork, loves the heft of it, so beautifully balanced. She begins pushing around a piece of prosciutto, being careful not to tine-scrape the elegant china ware.

Martina stops groaning long enough to demand of her guest, "You know where Jerry was right now?" Her voice has an intensity that is mirrored in her rigid body, arms stiff at her sides. "At Random House," she shouts, spittle spraying from her lips. "They're going to publish a collection of my husband's short stories."

Jerry shakes his head. "No, Marti. No, dearest," he says. "They *were* going to, an hour ago. But not anymore. That's over." He looks around his apartment. "That's over."

Elizabeth sits silently, recalling what she had intended to say to her former teacher—the caustic speeches, the pissed-off accusations of plagiarism, the 'How could you?' the 'What were you thinking?' None of that seems to matter anymore.

Jerry straightens in his chair. He places both palms on the table, exhales. "I'll return *The Criterion's* thousand dollar prize money. I'll call Mei Mei Chen and Random House, and I'll go to the Y, tell them I can't teach the workshops anymore."

Martina covers her mouth to stifle a scream that will not be stifled. It erupts, full-throated, as if she has just discovered that her newly birthed infant has emerged stillborn. She strikes her forehead with a fist. "Bastard." Then again. "Bastard." A third time. "You bastard." She turns and shambles into the kitchen. As soon as the door swings shut, explosive sobs are heard.

Elizabeth stands. "Jerry. Listen to me. It's Friday. Don't do anything today. Let's the three of us take the weekend and think about what we'll do. I'll call you Monday afternoon. Okay?"

He is staring through the French doors. "I guess," he says. "I guess."

Wednesday evening. A torrential rain is pelting Manhattan, making the streets barely passable. Despite the deluge, the auditorium at the 63rd Street YMCA is packed.

Mei Mei Chen, *The New Yorker's* literary editor, has been speaking about Jerry Dressler, regaling the crowd with anecdotes about one of the city's most beloved and influential creative writing teachers. She singles out in the audience some of the young writers Jerry has helped. She says that besides being a wonderful writing *teacher,* Jerry had honed his craft so finely that Random House will soon publish *Crosstown Buses and Other Stories.* And then, with a catch in her throat . . .

"A hideous accident . . . Jerry slipping from a ladder and falling to his death last Sunday while building shelves on his balcony. A tragic loss," Mei Mei Chen concludes, putting a lovely, finishing touch to the celebration of the author's life.

The author's widow is sitting in the front row and is soon surrounded by well-wishers, showering her with words of consolation, regret, and praise for her husband.

Elizabeth Ferragamo, standing alone in the rear of the hall, turns and quickly leaves the building.

Outside, if possible, it's raining even harder.

#

The Good Samaritan

CLAYTON CARLYLE HATED going to Harlem. Factories spewing out smoke. Semis pulling in and out from loading docks and crowding smaller vehicles off the road. Kids running all over the place. And a different set of people. Way too different. Not his kind.

But here he was, just past three o'clock on a muggy Thursday afternoon, in his shiny, new Nissan Pathfinder, waiting at the light at the corner of Lenox Avenue and 131st. He was on his way to Dyno-Mar Textiles, one of his firm's clients. The company's owner, Shaneequa Johnson, was waiting to review a set of contracts he was bringing to her. Dyno-Mar was expanding into Queens and Carlyle's law firm, Sooby Whattem Gluck, was handling the paperwork.

That morning, the lawyer had expressed his unhappiness with this assignment to his boss, Thornton Sooby. "For crying out loud, Thorny. Why don't you send Lavar? He knows the ropes up there. After all, Lavar's . . ." Clayton left the rest unsaid.

Sooby frowned at the associate attorney. "Go on up to Harlem, Clay. Put the contract in front of the woman. Have her sign. Come on back. Won't take half an hour. No biggie."

'No biggie?' Clayton thought. *Right. Easy for Sooby to say. He wouldn't be caught dead above 110th, top end of the Park.*

His appeal denied, the attorney went to his apartment and changed clothes. He shucked off suit and tie and donned a light summer shirt and Dockers. He hoped not to attract attention. Or at least, not stand out.

Just as the Lenox Avenue light turned green, an older, faded orange step van, speeding from Clayton's left, flew through the intersection, clipped the front end of a next-lane-over Subaru, spun out of control, and slued into a lamppost, catty-corner from the SUV.

The lawyer had instinctively mashed his brakes and was now frozen into a shuddering inaction. He had avoided being t-boned by a nano-second. Breathing deeply to steady his nerves, Clayton stared at the crashed step van, smoke billowing out of its front end. The driver's side door, facing the intersection, was shoved open. A woman, a *white* woman, a young, slender, and very attractive blond in tan shorts and a bright red t-shirt staggered out and crumpled against the side of the van. She seemed dazed and looked around desperately, as if in expectation of help arriving.

Clayton was about to run to her to lend assistance when a second vehicle, a grimy, older four-door Toyota sedan, screeched to a stop in the center of the intersection, twenty feet in front of his SUV. Two black men vaulted out and ducked behind the Toyota. One, a huge man, dressed in baggy shorts and a tattered pullover, dreadlocks cascading over his shoulders, carried a large handgun, which he now aimed over the hood of his car, pointing in the woman's direction. He shouted something at her, something Clayton could not make out.

The woman dashed around the van just as the man, *incredibly*, began firing, once, twice, three times, the bullets thudding into the side of her still-smoking wreck.

The second black man, skinny and naked to the waist, with a do-rag under a reverse-facing Mets baseball cap, spoke briefly to the first man, then rose up and began firing a pump action shot gun into the step van. The noise was deafening.

Clayton, wide-eyed and trembling, looked around him. Other drivers were crouching behind their cars, while a handful of pedestrians had taken refuge in back of a parked cab.

The attorney was terrified for himself *and* for the woman. She was obviously in danger of being shot to death by these two men. *I've got to do something!* he thought. He put his SUV into Drive, stamped down on the accelerator, and aimed the vehicle directly at the two shooters.

They never saw him coming. The SUV's front bumper caught them both in the back and crushed them against their Toyota.

Clayton sat there, stunned, staring through his windshield at the two bodies squashed over the blood-spattered hood of the Toyota. The lawyer wondered whether his insurance would cover the damage to his SUV's front end.

And then, a flash of scarlet and brown as the woman dashed from behind the step van and disappeared around the corner. Sirens filled the air.

Clayton Carlyle was arrested that afternoon and charged with two counts of manslaughter in connection with the deaths of Detective James Burgess of the NYPD's Major Crimes Division, and Sergeant Lewis Bellamy, 87th Precinct. The two police officers were killed in the line of duty while in pursuit of Renata Scarnecki, wanted for kidnapping, extortion, heroin trafficking, and arson. The Good Samaritan is looking at a ten spot for each count.

#

First Place, Second Place

January 18, 1933

"YOU'RE CERTAIN SHE'S going to be there," he asked. "You know that for a fact?"

"That's what Martin told me," she answered. "He said he heard it from Sally Astor. Sally told Martin the old lady is down from . . . just a second, let me think. Some place upstate, near Saranac Lake. Lennox or Lennon. Something like that."

The woman—delicately boned, pale skinned, in her mid-thirties with bobbed, curly red hair and hazel eyes—spoke with a soft Gulf Coast accent. Wearing only a sheer slip, she was seated at her dressing table in front of a mirror, bottles of cosmetics, tubes of creams randomly scattered before her. Using the first two fingers of her right hand, she carefully massaged a light peach colored rouge onto her cheeks. With the other hand, she reached out for a wine glass perched on the lip of her dressing table. She took a long swallow, finishing the drink.

"Supposed to be in town for a month or two," she said. "Visiting her niece . . . or somebody . . . staying close by, in the East 80s. Sally was certain the old lady would be making an appearance tomorrow night at Helen Vanderbilt's."

The woman broke off from the exclusive regard of herself and looked at her husband's reflection as he stood in back of her. His cummerbund, securely wrapped around his midriff, made his thin body appear even more slight. He placed a mostly-drained snifter of bourbon on her dressing table and began wrestling with a pair of gold, heart shaped cuff links, trying to fit them into stiffly pressed shirt sleeves. He managed the right cuff, but gave up on the left when his fingers succumbed to a bout of the shakes. He let both hands fall to his sides and stared down at the floor.

The woman paused in the application of a pale red lipstick. "What are you worried about, Scotty? I hear she's a decent sort. A bit severe, perhaps, but not a bad old girl. At least that's what Sally says." The woman took the man's unfinished drink and tossed the remains down in a single gulp.

Her husband raised his eyes to stare at her reflection. His face seemed to her aged and ashen.

The young woman swiveled around and extended both hands out to him. "Scotty, darling. For God's sake, dear. Get a grip."

Wrapped in a dark blue morning dress, buttoned to the neck, a woman in her early seventies was reading in her hosts' small library. She was sitting in a deeply cushioned armchair, a wool afghan spread over her lap and legs. She held a slim volume in one hand, smiling as she read, nodding and laughing occasionally. The chair backed up to a large, south-facing window that allowed the light from the late morning winter sun to shine onto the pages of her book. Without lifting her gaze, she adjusted the afghan and then nudged her wire frame glasses higher onto the bridge of her nose.

The door to the room opened and a much younger woman came in, carrying a tray.

"You look like you're thoroughly enjoying yourself," she said to the woman by the window, setting the tray down on an oval table in the center of the room. "I've brought some lovely tea. Oolong, I believe cook said. Will you have a cup?"

The older woman placed the open book face down on her lap. She removed her glasses and allowed them to hang by their silver chain.

The younger woman began laying out sugar, lemon, and milk. "Is that the book you've been looking for? What's it called? Something about a dance, I think."

"'*Save Me the Waltz,*'" the older woman said, holding up the novel and showing the binding and front cover. "She really writes beautifully. Certainly with more insight into the human condition than *he's* ever shown. And clearly with more emotion." The older woman inserted a tasseled bookmark, closed the novel, and placed it on a nearby end table. "In all honesty, I believe *she's* the better writer. Why the critics continue to call *him* 'America's greatest living author,' I've *never* understood." The older woman gathered up the afghan and folded it neatly on her lap. "Where *his* dialog always seems to me . . . I don't know. Somehow false. Forced. *Her* characters—and this is her *very* first book, mind you—they speak with an immediacy that's fresh, authentic." The older woman regarded the tray. "Yes, my dear. I'd love a cup of tea. One sugar, no lemon. No milk, please."

The younger woman poured, and with tongs, secured a cube of sugar and dropped it into the bone china cup. "You were searching for a copy of the novel for so long," she said. "Where did you finally find it?"

The older woman took the cup and set it carefully on top of the folded afghan, still on her lap. "Actually, it came in the mail," she said, sampling her tea. "Delicious, my dear. Oolong, you said?"

The next day, January 19, 1933

F. Scott Fitzgerald was in his library, stretched out on a brown leather sofa, a pair of small pillows propped under head and shoulders. Two empty tumblers rested on an end table, while another glass, half full of a golden liquid, was balanced on his chest. Fitzgerald was reading *The Age of Innocence*, by Edith Wharton. He found he could manage only a few pages at a time before he needed to go back and re-read—savoring certain phrases, sentences, passages, sometimes whole pages. He thought the writing as near to perfect prose as anything he had ever encountered. As he was trying to analyze the subtle way Wharton revealed the inner lives of the novel's three main characters, Fitzgerald's wife, Zelda, breezed into the room.

"Hello, darling," she smiled sunnily at him, removing her snow-dusted beaver coat and tossing it over an armchair. "Golly, the weather outside is simply delicious. Sally and I walked the entire length of Central Park. Then we grabbed a cab down to Max's for lunch. Saw Ruby and Buzzy there. They asked about you. Wondering what you've been up to."

With one hand, the young woman balanced herself against a shelf of books set into the wall, and with the other, wedged off fur-lined high boots, still partially covered with snow.

"Ruby says she's been waiting *years* for your next book. Says she hoped it would be a sequel to *Gatsby*. I told her you're hard at work, but I didn't tell her on what." Zelda walked to the fireplace and sat down on an ottoman next to the granite hearth. She parted the chain link screen and leaned forward toward the pile of low burning logs. Reaching toward the heat, she rubbed her palms together and looked back at her husband. "Still reading *The Age of Innocence?* Must be engaging. You've been at it for a week now."

Scott Fitzgerald took the glass off his chest, rose into

a sitting position, swallowed the rest of the drink, and placed the empty in a row next to its two mates. He avoided his wife's eyes and stared into the fire.

Zelda got up and joined him on the sofa, sitting so that their thighs touched. She leaned softly against her husband. "Is it *that* good, darling?"

Fitzgerald readjusted himself so that there were now a few inches between himself and his wife. He hesitated before answering, then in a quiet voice finally managed, "It's better than good, Zee. I mean, they don't give Pulitzers for bad writing." He glanced over at the three tumblers, reached for the end one, and held it up to his eyes. The light from the fire bounced off the remaining drops of amber in the bottom of the glass. He sipped down what was left of the drink, then returned the glass to its place. "I knew the book was going to be special," he said. "But I never realized just *how* special. That's probably why I've avoided it all these years."

Zelda regarded her husband as he let his head drop onto the back of the sofa, eyes closed. The occasional crackling of the fire was the only sound in the room.

Scott Fitzgerald breathed in deeply. "It's simply perfect. Not a Single. Wasted. Word. It's like . . . Medea. Or Oedipus. It's . . . beyond tragic. Yet so human at the same time." He sat upright and looked at his wife. "From the opening paragraph, the entire book is suffused with a presentiment of desperation and foredoom. Wharton never really comes out and says 'this story will not end happily.' But the reader knows, and can't help being caught up. It's simply brilliant."

Zelda took her husband's left hand in both of her own and began rubbing it gently. "When you meet her tonight at the Vanderbilts', you should tell her that. She'd be *so* pleased.

Hearing such a compliment from America's greatest author. What's the phrase? '*Praise from Caesar is praise indeed.*'"

He smiled back at her a thin 'thank you.' "I don't think I'll be going," he announced, brusquely disengaging himself from his wife, getting up, and shuffling in stockinged feet to the hearth. He faced the fire, hands in pockets, shoulders hunched.

Zelda watched his back for a moment then rose and walked across the room to a small table next to a set of floor-to-ceiling windows, heavily curtained against the winter chill. She reached down for a filigreed silver box, opened it, found a cigarette, tapped it on the metal case, and searched for a lighter. Finding none, she walked back to the fireplace, carefully moved her husband aside, and knelt down onto the hearth. She held the cigarette close to a glowing ember until it caught, then sat back on her heels, taking a long inhalation. She blew the smoke away over her shoulder, then slowly stood and reached to caress her husband's cheek. "Alright," she said. "We don't have to go. I'll call Sally and tell her to make excuses for us."

"You go," he insisted, barely audibly. "You don't have to miss out because I'm not brave enough to face an old woman. You go. I heard Carole Lombard and Gable are going to be there."

"Edith. Wharton is an *absolute* sweetheart," Zelda Fitzgerald reported, sitting again before her dressing table mirror, a thick terry cloth bathrobe draped around her shoulders. She was using tissues to cleanse a pasty layer of cold cream off her face, pausing now and then to take sips from a glass of white wine. "She said she was *'sorely disappointed'* you couldn't make it." Zelda spun around to face her husband.

"Her words, darling: *'sorely disappointed.'*" Zelda turned back to the mirror and resumed her nightly ritual, speaking to his reflected image.

"Seriously Scotty. She was very, *very* sweet. And quite a traveler, too. Said she's just come back from Paris and talked about the American community there. Sounded such fun. Said she thought the place was made for someone whose writing *'sparkled'* like yours." Zelda dabbed lightly at her chin, then tossed the used tissue onto a pile and gave her face one last inspection. Satisfied, she searched until she found a small bottle of pills, partially hidden under the pile of discarded tissues. She popped a pair of tablets into her mouth and washed them down with a long swallow of wine.

"Sparkled?" Scott Fitzgerald said, smiling, pleased.

"That's the exact word she used, darling, *"Sparkled,"* his wife answered. She stood, untied her bathrobe and let it drop to the floor. Dressed only in panties, Zelda walked to their bed, took a cigarette pack from under her lamp, shook one out and lit up.

"Who else was there?" her husband asked, moving and making room as his wife climbed under the covers.

"Lombard, but no Gable," she said. "Carole had a bit much to drink and started telling stories about her courtship with Clark. Really, Scotty, you should have been there taking notes."

Ashes from Zelda's cigarette dropped onto their down comforter. She ignored them. Scott Fitzgerald reached over and brushed them off.

"Then Chaplin and Paulette Goddard popped in for a minute. God, she's half his age and they're living together. He does like them young, doesn't he?" Zelda reached over and turned out her bed lamp. "And this dashing actor, Harry Cooper, the one who was in *The Virginian*. He was there, too."

"Not Harry, Zee. It's Gary. *Gary* Cooper was in *The Virginian*."

"Yes, that's it, darling. *Gary* Cooper. Tall and gorgeous. My God, gorgeous. Tallulah saw him first and just about had his clothes off before supper. They left midway through the meal." Zelda leaned over her night table and crushed her cigarette into an ashtray. She lay back in bed, pulling the comforter up to her chin. "Then at dinner, this lovely young actress . . . never seen her before . . . began telling about the most *outrageous* movie she was making. Seems there's an enormous ape that's captured and brought here to Manhattan. She says she gets grabbed by the beast and dragged to the top of the Empire State Building. Have you ever? We were all in shock. I don't quite remember her name. Begins with an F. Flo or Fran, or something. Faye, maybe. Yes, that's it. Faye. Are parents still naming their children Faye? God help us," Zelda yawned.

A week later, January 25, 1933

F. Scott Fitzgerald was stuck, been stuck for eight years, since 1925 and the publication of *The Great Gatsby*. He'd basked for long months in the notoriety the novel had won for him, milking the acclaim heaped on him by every critic in the nation. He'd temporarily suspended his other writing projects while on tour promoting the jazz age memoir and assumed —incorrectly, he came to realize—that he'd be able to jump back into his work at some point. But when the huzzahs had died down, he found himself bereft of inspiration. True, he'd been able to publish several short stories, many well received. But as far as an idea for a novel? Not a glimmering. His publishers had paid him a handsome advance toward that next work and needed constant putting off.

Fitzgerald had searched wide for the seeds of a story, for a useful theme. He began by reviewing his own large catalog of still unfinished works, hoping to find something he might continue. Nothing.

He consulted *'The Thirty Six Dramatic Situations,'* a French book of the previous century that divided the plots of every genre of literature into three dozen distinct categories. Again, no help.

The author thought to take example from his own life. But that idea was stillborn. With a sense of deep and unspoken resentment, Fitzgerald recalled how his wife Zelda, in confinement the year before because of a troubling mental condition, had written and had published—unbeknownst to him—her *own* novel, rich in the anecdotes of their two lives. A novel that used—and squandered, he thought—some of the choicest incidents, the most poignant possibilities, the most fascinating characters from their shared past. The modest regard the critics had extended to *Save Me The Waltz* was made doubly bitter when those same critics wondered what had happened to Zelda's husband—caught perhaps in some extended writer's block, they speculated. *Bastards!*

So, here he was. Eight years after *Gatsby*. Hounded by his publishers. The world growing more and more impatient, waiting for *'America's most acclaimed writer'* to get off his uncreative ass and produce something.

Now, dressed in tux and tails, he slouched against one of the thick, round marble pillars that supported the domed roof of the lobby of the Metropolitan Opera House in midtown Manhattan.

He and Zelda had come for Carmen, but his wife's very vocal and too loud disappointment with a much-heralded Swedish soprano caused them to flee their box just as the first act was ending. He steered her to the lobby and managed to get her to drink a cup of black coffee at the start of the opera's fifteen minute *entr'acte*.

Quieter now but only marginally more sober, Zelda was holding court on the other side of the crowded foyer.

Left alone, Fitzgerald went to the bar, stood elbow to elbow with other tuxedoed men, and ordered a double bourbon, on the rocks. He took a long swallow just as the chimes began to sound, calling the audience back to their seats for the second act. He watched across the room as his wife said her several goodbyes. But then surprisingly, she took the hand of an older woman and began leading her toward him. For a bare moment, Fitzgerald was unsure who this other person might be. Then it came to him. Though he had never met Edith Wharton and had only the vaguest idea what she looked like, he was certain, beyond a doubt, that he was about to meet the author whose novel, *The Age of Innocence,* had won the 1921 Pulitzer Prize for Literature, beating out his very own, his precious, his first great success, his *This Side of Paradise.*

The two women, now arm in arm, wound their way through the lobby toward the 1921 Pulitzer Prize for Literature Runner-up. The ladies were smiling hugely. Though answering their smiles was the last thing he thought his face could do, Fitzgerald forced the corners of his mouth to rise. He quickly drained the rest of his bourbon, put the glass on the bar, and turned again to the ladies, now just a few paces away.

Still holding the other woman by the arm, Zelda reached out and took her husband's hand, drawing him closer. "Scotty darling. I'd like you to meet Mrs. Edith Wharton. Mrs. Wharton, this is my husband, Scott Fitzgerald."

"At last," said Edith Wharton, extending her right hand to him. "I am *so* pleased to meet you, Mr. Fitzgerald. I was looking forward to it last week at Mrs. Vanderbilt's, but when I arrived, I learned from your dear wife of your *horribly* painful toothache. I do hope you've recovered."

While maintaining his death-masque smile, Fitzgerald reluctantly but dutifully shook the offered hand. He was surprised both by the strength of her grip and by the beauty of her fingers. He conjured an image of her with a ream of paper stacked neatly nearby, lovely fingers churning out page after gorgeously written page of exquisite prose. He dropped his hold on her hand as soon as he was able and glanced at his wife. She smiled at him, happy her invented excuse had been successful.

"Glad to meet you, too," Fitzgerald was able to get out. "I'm quite . . . quite recovered, thank you, Mrs. Wharton. Damnable toothache put me right on my back." A pause. Silence. He looked to his wife to keep the conversation going. But Zelda's interests were being drawn elsewhere. She stepped around her husband and advanced toward the bar.

Fitzgerald noticed with alarm that his wife was reaching for a glass of something. Actually half a glass—obviously someone else's partially finished drink—a rum-looking, fruity concoction with a miniature parasol and a bright red swizzle stick poking up beyond the rim of a tall goblet.

Edith Wharton joined Fitzgerald in staring at Zelda as

she swirled the glass in her hand, causing the ice within to tinkle quietly. With a forefinger, she moved the parasol and swizzler aside, downed the drink, licked her lips delicately, and carefully returned the empty glass to the bar, its original owner, apparently, none the wiser. She turned back to her husband, her smile now slightly askew. "Scotty, darling. I was just telling Mrs. Wharton how much you enjoyed reading *The Age of Innocence.*" Zelda turned to the woman by her side. "It's true Mrs. Wharton. It's taken Scotty years to getting 'round to reading it, but he literally could *not* put it down. Could you, darling?" she concluded, looking brightly at her husband.

Fitzgerald took a half step backward and stared mutely at his wife. He searched for an appropriate comment, but found that his tongue seemed to have frozen into a solid lump. The best he could do was to resurrect the rictus of his first, 'Glad-to-meet-you-too,' smile.

"Scotty spent most of last week reading your novel, Mrs. Wharton. I could hardly get him to the dinner table."

Fitzgerald noted with dismay that his wife's voice had regained the slurry cadence with which she had so roundly and loudly vilified the soprano during Carmen's *Habanera,* the singer's Act One solo.

Wharton, however, could not have seemed happier at this latest revelation. "I can't tell you, Mr. Fitzgerald, how pleased that makes me," she said, wondering to herself at the same time just how much balm she might need to soothe the man's obviously bruised ego. She decided that his self-esteem needed propping up. She gently touched his forearm. "I recall when you and I were in competition for the Pulitzer, twelve years ago. I thought for certain the committee was going to award *you* the prize for your sublime *This Side of Paradise.* I thought my own effort paltry and lacking compared to the elegance of *your* writing."

Zelda beamed at her husband, an I-told-you-so look in her raised eyebrows.

"And then, several years ago," Wharton continued, "when the Pulitzer committee *again* overlooked you, well, I was tempted to write to them. Imagine," she said with a growing, if not wholly authentic, sense of indignation, "giving the prize to that awful Sinclair Lewis for that monumentally boring *Arrowsmith.* And consigning your superb *Gatsby* to second tier status. Unconscionable!"

The two-time Pulitzer Runner-up could only nod and shrug his shoulders. He was unsure what he had conveyed to the winner of the prize with the shrug, but at this stage in the conversation, he didn't really give a damn.

"And you, my dear," Wharton said to Zelda. "I must tell you that I just finished reading *your* perfectly wonderful novel. For a first effort it was quite remarkable. Thank you so much for mailing it to me."

At this news, the muscles in Scott Fitzgerald's jaw began a rhythmic grinding. *Another betrayal*, he thought. Not only had his wife used—misused, he fully believed—the material he had been saving for *his* next novel, but she had sent to Edith Wharton, probably, he imagined, with a *"See, I can write, too,"* dedication.

"Mr. Fitzgerald, it must be deeply gratifying knowing how well your wife's first book has turned out. I do hope you'll encourage her to keep up with her writing," Edith Wharton said, smiling at Fitzgerald. But with a sudden sense of alarm, the Pulitzer winner noted that the Pulitzer runner-up had begun to rock back and forth on his heels, fists clenched at his sides. He was staring at his wife in a way that made the older woman shudder.

When America's most esteemed author could not make a cogent reply, Edith Wharton rushed to mollify the apparently thin-skinned and jealous novelist. She blurted out, "Mr. Fitzgerald. I'll be in town for another few weeks. Perhaps we could meet for lunch." She searched for a compelling reason for the invitation. "I'm having a bit of trouble organizing my current work." She could have kicked herself right then and there. To confess to this man—this upstart, this second rater—her own composing problems seemed to her an unbearably stupid act. But in for a penny, in for a pound, she told herself, soldiering on. "I would be most pleased to accept any advice you might give . . . suggestions . . . directions," she trailed off.

Somewhere in F. Scott Fitzgerald's liquor-addled brain, a teeny light went off. The muscles at the corners of his mouth relaxed. His tongue thawed, and he was able to smile. "That would be lovely, Mrs. Wharton. I'll look forward to it."

Two weeks later, February 8, 1933

The lunch crowd at the Russian Tea Room had come and gone. In a far corner, in a window booth that looked out onto 57th Street, the winner and the runner-up for the 1921 Pulitzer Prize for Literature sat opposite each other, coffee and wedges of the watering hole's famous cheese cake before them. The younger man smoked, the older woman fiddled with a pad of paper and a finely made gold fountain pen.

"Well, I've managed to avoid talking about the reason

I've asked you to lunch . . ." Wharton glanced at her watch ". . . for almost a full hour." She smiled somewhat sheepishly across the table.

Fitzgerald returned her smile. "Take your time, dear Mrs. Wharton," he said, sampling the cheese cake.

The woman sat back in the booth and gathered herself. "I've an idea for a novel, Mr. Fitzgerald," she said, putting the cap back on her pen and closing her note pad. "The idea was given to me, rather unwittingly, by a young woman I met on the train from Albany, about a month ago. We shared a compartment. She appeared to me to be quite distraught. I enquired after her health. She said she was 'fatigued.' We took tea and she seemed to regain some strength. Her name is Rose Lynholm. From the Midwest somewhere. Milwaukee, if I recall. But I believe she was raised in France. A beautiful young thing, very fragile. I suppose because of my age and the fact that she was familiar with my work, she seemed to trust me."

Edith Wharton hesitated, stirring her coffee absentmindedly. "It seems the young woman is a quite successful actress. She's been in films you've undoubtedly seen. One with the Barrymores, in fact. Well, about five years ago, she traveled to France, to the Riviera. She met a man, a married man, and began a secret affair. He's a psychiatrist, an American with his own clinic in Vienna. His wife had originally been one of his patients, a woman who had been brutally sexually abused by her father. A horrible, ghastly story. She and the doctor eventually married and had two children. Somehow—I believe through a friend of theirs, a drunk, by the way—she discovered the affair her husband was having with Marie. The wife, still psychologically vulnerable, had a breakdown and threatened suicide. The husband made amends and Marie dropped out of the picture. At least, for a while. She returned to Hollywood. Two years passed. Then, just a few months ago, Marie bumped into the man, here in New York. He'd come back to America for his father's funeral. His life had taken a turn for the worse. His marriage was over. His wife had left him for another man. He was drinking heavily. He and Marie picked up where they'd left off, but after only a few weeks—a rather awful few weeks, according to Marie—he vanished, without a word. She felt cast aside once again. She told me she thought the man was deeply in love with her and she felt devastated by his disappearance." Edith Wharton sat back. A shiver of disquiet ran through her shoulders.

Sensing the end of the narrative, Scott Fitzgerald let his gaze drop to his clasped hands, resting on the white tablecloth in front of him.

Edith Wharton took a sip of coffee. "I'm unsure, Mr. Fitzgerald, what course of action I should take with this tale. On the one hand, I fear I'd be betraying Marie's confidence by somehow refashioning it into something literary. Something from which I might profit. On the other hand, I find her story so compelling. So mystifying and unresolved."

Fitzgerald let several seconds pass. He glanced out the window to a clamorous 57th Street. "Mrs. Wharton, your loyalty to this young woman's trust in you is commendable. Yet, I feel as you do, as you *must*. This is a story that really begs telling." He paused. "Have you begun to put it to paper?"

"Only the barest of outlines so far," Edith Wharton said. "I even have a title, tentative, still somehow elusive, not quite right."

"What are you calling it?"

"*Gentle is the Night*," Edith Wharton answered.

"An evocative title," America's most accomplished writer said, signaling to the waiter for the check.

#

The Surprise Artist

ROSALIND HOFFMAN, A willowy, green-eyed, sweetly-dispositioned, thirty-six-year-old was abandoned by her husband Friedrich in February 2005.

Herr Hoffman, a senior accountant at Deutsche Bank Filiale on Munich's Herterrich Strasse, ran off with Gerta, his two decades younger secretary.

Since their marriage had been on a southerly journey for several years, Rosalind was neither shocked nor particularly affronted when she learned she had been two-timed.

A very large divorce settlement allowed the betrayed wife to purchase a sturdily constructed, three-story Munich home, built in 1867 for a mistress of Richard Wagner.

The structure was located in a residential cul-de-sac and was within bicycling distance of the Max Planck Institut. It was there that Rosalind had graduated with high honors at the age of twenty, earned her PhD in string theory at twenty-four, and was then hired the next year as a researcher and teacher of physics.

Her family life—she and her two daughters, Monique and Karla—was *not* made more difficult with the departure of Herr Hoffman. The opposite, in fact. Because as soon as Freddy was no longer in the picture, Grandma Hilda, Rosalind's mother, moved in and pretty much took over the maintenance of the place—cooking, cleaning, and tending the huge backyard garden.

Life proceeded without incident for several years, but hit a bump towards the end of summer 2012. One brilliantly sunny day in June, with a cradling breeze blowing off the River Isar, Hilda decided enough was enough. She sat herself in her favorite chair at garden's edge, lifted her head to the warming sun, and let the life pass out of her.

Because Hilda had been a rabid collector all her life—never missing an estate sale, regularly visiting second hand stores—it took Rosalind six months to work up the energy to have a look through her mother's many possessions. Sort things out. Save some memories. Toss some.

All of it—the good, the bad, the unknown—had been stored in the attic when the matriarch first moved in and had been gathering dust ever since.

One morning in mid-January, near the end of winter break, Rosalind climbed up to the attic and began rummaging through her mother's things. A thin light filtered through dormer windows as snow collected on the sills.

By the end of that first day, Rosalind had amassed a huge pile of 'tossables,' a hodge-podge of items Hilda had collected from God-knows-where. The 'saveable' pile, although considerably smaller, was filled with memories Rosalind could not, would not abandon: a sachet of her mother's that still retained the barest scent of lavender; a Christmas wreath woven from birch branches, adorned with red ribbon; a copy of her mother's marriage license to Georg Stenholm—a Swede who was in Bavaria on a summer hiking vacation in 1948, met Hilda, and proposed the next day.

After hauling down the discards, Rosalind began to organize her mother's memories. She bought expandable folders, storage boxes, and a three-drawer filing cabinet.

At the end of the fourth day, she thought she was done, her mother's most treasured items sorted, preserved, catalogued. A final search of the attic, however, brought a surprise: stuck behind a rafter, cloaked in spider webs, Rosalind discovered a small wooden box, about the size of a loaf of pumpernickel. The two heavy, metal hasps were in good working order and had kept the top of the box snugly closed. Rosalind opened it with care. Inside, she found five envelopes, all unsealed and each containing a single piece of paper. Each envelope was addressed to someone with the initial E. And none showed a sender's name.

But now the attic was darkening with the end of the day. There'd be no time to examine the contents of the envelopes as her daughters were due home any time and needed to eat before their evening soccer practice. Rosalind closed the box and carried it downstairs to her office.

The next day was Rosalind's long day at work. She taught an undergraduate course in single variable calculus until ten, then the weekly faculty lunch, followed by an afternoon in her lab with four doctoral candidates who were helping her prepare a lecture in micro-fluids. At five, a meeting with two colleagues to discuss and finalize a paper they were hoping to publish in *Annalen der Physik.* It would be their first submission to that grand and glorious journal and they wanted to make absolutely certain that *"The Photoelectric Effect Re-examined: Planck, Einstein, and Compton"* was as tightly argued as the three of them could manage. Though her two colleagues were confident that the piece was ready, Rosalind had a few niggling doubts about this phrase, that point.

"Come on, Rosa," they urged her. "It's ready. Let's submit it." But Rosalind dallied.

She didn't get home from work until after nine. The house was quiet, the girls, upstairs, hopefully hard at their studies.

As usual, the scientist went first to her office to check

her email. Nothing vital, nothing that couldn't wait. Hand on the chain of her desk lamp, she glimpsed the box. She cleared away a space on her desk, brought the box over and set it gently down, as if sensing it might contain something fragile, something precious. She opened it and took out the first of the five envelopes. It was almond white and was the size and shape usually used for birthday or anniversary cards. On the front, 'to E' was written in an older print style, blocky, no serifs. *A masculine hand,* Rosalind thought. And since there was no postmark, she assumed it had been hand-delivered.

She opened the envelope and withdrew a single sheet of light blue paper, folded once. She placed the page on her desk and smoothed it open.

A poem. Written, it appeared, by the same hand that had inscribed the E on the envelope. And a date in the upper right, *May 1931.*

The handwriting style jumped out at her. It was severely slanted with some letters written in a way that was almost out of fashion by 1931.

The poem's rhyme scheme was a simple ABAB. But the simplicity of the structure belied the subtle beauties within. Rosalind slowly read the three-stanza poem. And again. Then once more. Each time, the words took on a slightly nuanced meaning. Each line seemed to Rosalind to be a universe unto itself, a string of words perfectly phrased and sonorously rhymed.

She had always maintained an intense interest in German literature, especially poetry. In her final year at gymnasium, Rosalind had received a commendation for a well-researched paper on the mutual influences, one on the other, of Goethe and Schiller. That interest in literature carried over at university into her major study—physics. She often told her mother that she felt the arts and the sciences were simply two sides of the same coin, each peeling away the onion skin to gain further insight into the truth. And now, reading this exquisite poem by an unknown author, she felt again that same kinship between art and science.

Somehow, the poem gave her a fresh insight into the paper she and her colleagues were preparing for publication. She felt somehow reassured about those few parts where she had doubts. She decided she'd call her collaborators the next day and express to them her confidence in their joint effort and her readiness to call the research paper 'done.'

She looked again at the single piece of paper in front of her, turned it over, held it to the light, then re-examined the envelope, looking for something that might provide a clue to the author. There was nothing.

Because of the effect the poem had on her, she was sorely tempted to read more, to pick up the second envelope, to see if whatever it contained could match—*it couldn't exceed*, she thought—the elegiac contents of the first envelope.

But she purposely resisted the temptation and went once more to the first poem for a final re-reading. This time out loud.

The poem proposed a meeting with E, a very much-desired meeting on the part of the author who made neither promises nor declarations, but simply spoke about the effects E had on the writer, profound and unforgettable.

She folded the poem, returned it to its envelope, put the letter back into the box, shut the lid, and secured the hasps. She turned off her desk light, then hesitated. Sitting back in her chair, she wrapped Hilda's crocheted shawl around her shoulders and sat in the dark for another half hour, repeating to herself, over and over, the memorized first stanza. She fell asleep in the chair and dreamed of the photoelectric effect.

The following afternoon, Rosalind left work early. Arriving home, she shut off her cell phone and returned to her office. From four o'clock until Monique came storming into the house at five-thirty, shouting 'hello' to anyone who might shout back a greeting, Rosalind read the next four poems. They were dated from November, 1931, to January, 1934.

Each of the envelopes had either 'to E,' or simply 'E' on the outside. Inside, single sheets of light blue paper, and again three stanza poems.

Poems number two and three followed the same rhyming scheme—ABAB—as the first, from the night before. In poems four and five, however, the author chose an AABB rhyming scheme. Rosalind felt the change was an expression of the author's different mind-set. His longing, (if it were a 'he') so apparent in the first three poems, had evolved into something more firmly based, as if the relationship between E and the author had advanced to a higher, more secure stage.

She returned to the poems daily, unable *not* to read them. Like an addict, she craved the words.

Rosalind shared the contents of Hilda's box with her two daughters. They differed in their reaction the way siblings might differ. Monique admired the poems, thought they were sweet, nothing more. Karla loved them deeply and was at her mother's side whenever Rosalind sat down with the box. They would read the five poems to each other and would spend time speculating on the identity of both the author and E, his apparent *inamorata*. For that's what it must be, mother and daughter decided—a man writing to his beloved, fiancé, or spouse. They could not conceive of any other pairing.

By the middle of the spring term, Rosalind had memorized the five poems and was happy to recite them to anyone who would listen—mostly to her co-workers and students. For an entire week, she began her morning classes with a declamation of one of the five.

At first, faculty and students alike were puzzled. Their usually reserved colleague and teacher—someone given neither to verbal hyperbole nor physical demonstrativeness— had seemingly been transformed. And as she continued to declaim the poems, their power and beauty proved infectious. Several students asked for written copies. Their teacher was happy to oblige. Because she thought the old-fashioned script in which the originals were written was too difficult to read, Rosalind re-typed the poems rather than simply Xerox them.

She was often asked about the author, about E, about the 'when' and 'where' of the poems. She'd cite her mother's penchant for collecting and told them as much as she knew, or didn't know. The poems' origins remained a mystery.

Up until then, only she and her daughters had seen Hilda's originals. But when a friend, Gunther Adler, a lecturer in German Literature at the Ludwig-Maximilians-Universitat, learned of the poems and asked to read them, Rosalind readily agreed.

She and Gunther had known each other for years, were students together at gymnasium. He stopped by on a Saturday afternoon. They caught up over coffee and strudel, then went to Rosalind's study. He sat while she arrayed the five envelopes before him. He opened the top one, removed the piece of blue paper, stared at it, and froze, a stunned expression on his face.

Rosalind was jarred by his reaction. "What is it, Gunther? You look like you've seen a ghost."

"It might be worse," he said. "You're certain you have no idea who the author of these poems is."

"No. No idea. Why?" she asked, then lightly, "Are you telling me you recognize the handwriting?"

"Open your computer. Let's go online."

At the end of an hour of searching and comparing handwriting samples, Adler was certain he had matched the poems to their author.

Rosalind was thunderstruck, her world turned topsy-turvy. She slumped deep into her chair, shivering. The possibility that E was Eva Braun was almost too horrifying to contemplate.

#

Inflight

JACOB HUMPHRIES SAT cradled in his exit-row aisle seat, winging his way back to his home in Hilo. The veteran airline mechanic had spent the last four days in Los Angeles at a not very successful bargaining session with his employer, All West Air.

The union rep usually fell fast asleep as soon as he was in his seat and came awake only when he felt the landing gear descend.

But half way across the Pacific, an abrupt lurch, coupled with the captain's intercom admonition to, "Please buckle up as we expect some turbulence," brought him to a place between dreamland and dim consciousness.

He readjusted his six-foot frame in his seat, stretched his legs to their full extent, pulled his down vest closer around his neck, and sought to return to his blacked-out state.

But the next, much more severe jolt—an audible *'braaaak'* of fuselage and wings—rocked him into full wakefulness.

Although he kept his eyes tightly closed, his other senses jumped into high alert. He felt a rustling in the aisle. Certainly, he thought, the flight attendants battening down the hatches, reminding folks to strap in.

And along with the movement, Jacob also became aware of a low hum of voices, soft and business-like, as of a list being read.

"Yes. Here he is. Juan Carlos Cabrillo, from Oaxaca. Or however the hell you pronounce it. Check him off, Roberta."

"Got him, Bobby. How 'bout the Kowalchuks? I think they're yours, Andy, aren't they?"

"Right. Mother and daughter. Stephanie and Elizabeth. Wow, wouldya look at this! They're from Key West, no less.

I was down there fishing for marlin in '28, just before the market went tits up."

The weirdness of the last comment, spoken by someone standing right next to him, made Jacob straighten in his seat. Without shifting his body, he tilted his head slightly, slowly opened his right eye, and immediately slammed it shut. The plane was swarming with spectral figures, all dressed in white and black, ghostily floating above the seats, gliding up and down the aisles. Jacob couldn't help himself—his eyes bulged open and he sat bolt upright.

"The fuck is going on?" he demanded loudly.

An older woman in the aisle seat across from Jacob looked at him, revulsion showing in her turned-down mouth. "The language some people think they can get away with these days. Disgusting."

"But don't you see them?" he shouted at her.

She shook her head in a tsk-tsk gesture. "Drunk," she said under her breath.

Jacob now turned to the man sitting to his left, reading the Wall Street Journal. A child-ghost, dressed in white, was perched on his head.

Jacob realized he was the only one who could see the specters.

One of the images, a wonderfully attractive, mid-thirties Asian woman, dressed in a very smartly tailored black pants suit, black silk blouse, open to mid-chest, stopped what she was doing, did a double take, then wafted over to him. She quickly summoned another specter. "Judas," she hailed in a frenzied voice, "he can see us!"

A white-clad ghost floatingly changed course and headed for Jacob's seat. He clutched a rolled-up sheaf of papers, unscrolled it, and began a hasty read.

All the other ghostly shapes stopped what they were doing and began whispering to each other, looking and pointing in Jacob's direction.

"Yeah, I can see you," Jacob countered. "What's goin' on? Who the *hell* are you?"

"Who the *hell* am I?" asked the white-robed specter, looking up from the scroll-manifest. You may soon find out, like in . . . maybe . . ."

"Twenty-seven minutes to splat down," an eerie voice rattled through the cabin. "Whoopee," the voice added.

"Right. How 'bout in twenty-seven minutes, smart-ass," white robe said. "You just may discover who the *hell* I am."

Jacob's mouth suddenly went Gobi-dry, his tongue glued to his palate. At that moment, the crackling of the plane's intercom split the air.

"Folks, this is Captain Braackle. Our course has us heading into the outer fringes of Typhoon Tillie. We're gonna try and gain some altitude so's to miss most of the bumps. We may have a bit of turbulence, however, so we ask you all to please remain in your seats and stay buckled up. Thanks."

The Asian woman now signaled to another image several rows back. "Peter. Get over here. We've got an outlier." She turned to Jacob and rested her hand gently on his shoulder. "Please try and relax. We'll find out the problem, I'm certain." She looked down at him with large, luminous dark eyes and gave him an unexpectedly sensual smile. "You'll be fine," she said sweetly. She bent forward, allowing him full view into her blouse where beautifully sculpted breasts beckoned to him. "I'll take care of you. Promise," she whispered in his ear.

Jacob thought to take her hand. But just then, a short, rotund man of some fifty years, dressed in a Guns N' Roses t-shirt and black jeans glided up and came to rest directly on the seat in front of Jacob. "What's going on, Patty?" the man demanded.

"Peter, this gentleman seems to be an outlier. I'm not sure what we're supposed to do. I've never had an outlier before," Patty answered. She looked down at Jacob and gave him another deeply suggestive (he thought) smile. Her fingers lightly moved from his shoulder to the back of his neck. The feeling was like a low voltage Taser current, charging down his spine right into his pelvis where he felt a throbbing. Holy Cow!

"Impossible," Peter said, grabbing the scroll from Judas.

Peter rapidly scanned the manifest, checked the seat number, and looked around. "This seat was supposed to be empty," he squeaked. "How did you get here?" He stared accusingly at Jacob.

"Jesus H. Christ, I don't know. I just walked on. I work for the airline."

"Please," Patty said, firmly. "He really gets ticked off when you use his name like that."

Jacob stared at her. "Ticked off? Who gets ticked off?"

"Jesus, that's who. Christ."

Jacob took his head in his hands. "Oh. Yeah, right. That's just great." He looked up at her and with undisguised sarcasm, "I suppose you *know* him."

The woman bristled. "As a matter of fact, I had lunch with him and Mary M. last week. Lamb kabobs in pita. He likes to keep it simple. Old habits, I guess."

Jacob felt his head begin to throb.

"Nineteen minutes to impact," a diabolical voice echoed through the cabin. "Specters, take your places. Let's have some *fun*."

Peter turned to Patty and Judas. "L . . listen, I've got to make sure everything is ship shape," he stuttered nervously and wrung his hands. "Can you two handle the outlier? I mean, this *hardly* seems a problem." With that, Peter fled, flitting crazily toward the front of the aircraft.

Judas smirked as he watched the black clad specter depart. "It's the Peter Principle, writ large. Probably *named* for him. Promoted beyond his level of competence."

Patty wagged her head. "Supposed to have made his bones during the Reformation. He was Martin Luther's uncle, or something. But you're right, running the show tonight is definitely beyond his pay grade. They should have started him with something less catastrophic. The small fire in that hotel in Philly. Only six dead. *That* he could have handled. But . . . you know . . . He *does* have good intentions," she added, in Peter's defense.

"The road to hell . . ." the white-robed Judas leered at her.

Patty looked at him archly. "You of all people, ought to know."

Judas blanched. His shoulders slumped. He turned and glided away up the aisle, muttering to himself, "You betray one guy . . . ."

Jacob had been following the conversation closely. "That was Judas? *The* Judas?"

"One and only. Jesus has forgiven him a thousand times, but he can't forgive himself. Too bad. Lives in Hell."

"Lives in Hell? Literally? But he's wearing white.

Doesn't that mean he's in heaven?"

Patty smiled down at Jacob, reached over, and playfully mussed his hair. "You're really cute. No, actually, that color thing—the black and white thing—got flipped during the Fourth Crusade. Not sure how. But when you think about it, isn't it smarter to wear white in hot places? Reflect the heat?"

"Right. I didn't think of that," Jacob agreed. Then, tentatively, "Am I getting white or black? I mean, where the hell . . . er . . . where the heck am I going?"

"You want to know who decides where the soul goes, is that it?"

"Fifteen minutes to impact. Yee-ha!" someone shouted happily down the corridor.

"Fifteen minutes," Patty said. "Not a lot of time. Well, if you must know, Jake . . . I can call you Jake, can't I?"

"Sure. But . . . who decides?"

"The Decider, of course. And I don't mean your former dim-witted president. I don't know where he came up with that but the *real* Decider is totally pissed," Patty said, a touch of pique creeping into her voice. "Anyhow, the decision is made just hours before someone dies. Kinda fun guessing where people are gonna end up."

"How'd you die?" Jacob asked.

Patty shrugged. "My husband shot me. Four in the chest with a .357. Boy, did that sting."

"Whoa. Why'd he shoot you?"

"Caught me and my lover—the postman, wouldn't you guess—*in flagrante,* if you know what I mean. Classic pose. My legs straight up in the air." Patty smiled at the memory. "That was in '81. We were living in Portland. Hate that town.

So white, so perfect. Ick. Anyhow, he got the lethal needle. We work together once in a while, especially on major calamities. He was actually supposed to be here with us tonight, but got called away to a giant mud slide in Honduras. I heard over three hundred people got buried alive. What an *awful* way to go."

"Wait, wait, wait a minute," Jacob said. "I don't get it. Both of you broke God's . . . eh . . . the Decider's commandments. You were adulterous and he was a murderer. How come you both got to go to heaven?"

Patty looked at him indulgently. "Who's a saint, Jake?" she asked. "I mean, 'Which of us is without sin?' if I can quote Jesus. He's a great guy by the way. And can he tell a story. Even though I've heard it a dozen times, still makes me howl. Does this imitation of Pilate condemning Jesus. Says the story has gotten totally screwed up. It was actually Barabbas who was washing Pilate's *feet*. How it turned into what was written in Mark no one knows, but Jesus does this shtick—he plays Barabbas and he gets Peter O'Toole to play Pilate. So campy. I almost wet my pants."

"Heaven sounds fun," Jacob said.

"Don't be fooled. It's usually a total bore. Everyone tries to be so Goody-Miss-Two-Shoes. Preaching about divinity. Holier than thou. And those fundamentalists. The worst, with their, 'Love God or I'll kill you.' What hypocrites."

"I never dreamed it might be like that. I mean, all those Renaissance paintings. Cherubs, harp-playing angels."

"Don't believe it," she said. "I actually can't wait for those missions south, down to Hell, looking for souls to save. Now there's a fun place. Hell's one big party."

"But what about the heat? Hell fire? All that?"

"Hell fire? Baloney. Usually no hotter than a spring day in Vegas. And it's a dry heat. True, it never cools down, but still, if you can stand the heat, Hell's where you want to be. Though Satan's kinda uptight, especially after he comes back down from the surface. He can't stand it up top. Has poor circulation. Which is why the thermostat in Hell is always cranked way up."

"So how come all these stories about how great Heaven is and how awful a place Hell is? What's the deal?"

"Strictly propaganda. Keep the population on the surface from acting out."

At that moment, the aircraft was sucked into a wind shear and began plunging earthward. Everyone on board was now awake, buckled in, and holding on. No one was screaming. Yet. But there were audible prayers, many invoking God, Jesus, some people calling out to Elohim, and a pair of women in the seats in front of Jacob beseeching salvation from Allah.

Outside the plane, a moonless sky was illuminated by lightning flashes. Thunderclaps engulfed the entire aircraft and shook it violently.

With his new insight into eternity, Jacob sought to ease the fears of his fellow travelers. He turned around and spoke to a pair of women who seemed particularly frightened. "Don't worry," he assured them quietly, "We all have our guardian angels."

The younger of the two women looked at him venomously. "Screw you, buddy. Spare me that life-after-death bullshit."

A white-clad specter, sitting on the woman's shoulder, winked at Jacob. "Guess where she's going?" the image asked, chuckling.

Patty smiled. "Crazy isn't it? It's the same every time. They all want to go to heaven but none of them wants to die to get there. But don't worry," she added, beginning to massage Jacob's neck. "You'll be just fine." The effect of Patty's soothing fingers on him was immediate. Jacob had to shift in his seat to accommodate his bulging erection.

"Tell me something, Patty." Jacob hesitated, unconsciously licking his lips. "What about sex?"

She looked at him appreciatively. "Heavenly," she said. "Guys never lose their hard ons. Or is it hards on? Like attorneys general. Whatever. And we ladies . . . well, it's really quite wonderful. *Every* time," she said, brushing some lint off of her tailored suit. "Damn recirculated air. I hate flying anymore."

Jacob reached up and took Patty's hand. "Sounds super, but I'm worried. How do I get to heaven if I don't have my own specter? Why don't I have someone here, now, to watch over me?"

"No problem, Jake. The solution is simpler than you might think. If you have a spiritual interaction with one of the specters, with me, for instance, you'll be safe."

"What kind of spiritual interaction?" Jacob asked. "I mean. What am I supposed to do?"

Patty grinned, parked herself on his lap, and lightly stroked his cheek. "Remember when I described how I looked when I got caught *in flagrante?*"

The stirring in Jacob's pants now became an insistent throbbing. "Sure. You said you were caught with your legs straight up in the air. Right?"

"Right. Well . . ." Patty hesitated, smiling at him. "How

better to connect spiritually?"

Jacob gulped. "I like it. But wait a sec. I have a wife. I've never cheated on her. Twenty-three years."

"It wouldn't be cheating because you'll be dead in a few minutes. Then we'll be together. But not forever," she added quickly. "That's another myth we have trouble debunking. People come up all the time thinking it's forever. It's not. You're in for a thousand years—goes by like a second—then you get to be protoplasm on some Decider-forsaken planet, Decider-knows where. And you gotta wait another zillion years until consciousness blooms—if it ever does. But at least we'll have some time together."

A huge 'BOOM' wrapped itself around the plane, rattling the wings. The aircraft began a steep nose-first dive, spinning slightly. The voice of Captain Braackle came over the intercom but was an inaudible background to the outside thunder and the inside shrieking of the passengers. Braackle's warning to prepare for an emergency water landing was barely heard above the passengers screaming, "We're gonna diiiiie."

All of the black and white specters were now laughing hysterically, some wiping tears from their eyes.

"We don't have a lot of time, Jake," Patty said, rising, unbuttoning her slacks and letting them drop to the floor. Her panties followed. The woman's exquisite nether regions stared Jacob directly in the face. Despite the insanity of the situation, despite the shouting, screaming, praying, and sobbing of his fellow passengers, Jacob Humphries was mesmerized, fully loaded.

"God . . . eh . . . Decider. I am *so* ready," he said, undoing his own pants and shimmying them down to his ankles, followed quickly by his underwear. Patty threw a leg over the seated man and mounted him.

"This really is heaven," Jacob moaned, only momentarily distracted by the man in the next seat who had long ago discarded the WSJournal and after a moment's glance at the writhing, pumping, half-naked man next to him—having sex with thin air—resumed his wailing.

At about five thousand feet, the aircraft stopped spinning and oh-so-gradually came out of its dive.

Within sight of Waikiki, surfboarders gawked at the aircraft as it leveled off. A few minutes later, the plane landed safely at Honolulu International.

The mood in the cabin was mixed: the passengers were euphoric, hugging each other, crying happily, applauding the pilot, thanking the crew.

The feeling among the black and white specters, however, was decidedly glum. Judas went around bad mouthing Peter's handling of the whole affair. "That's what you get when you send an amateur to do a man's job," he complained.

Incredibly, among passengers and crew, there was only a single casualty. A fatality, in fact. An as yet unidentified man, sitting in one of the exit rows, had apparently suffered a heart attack. The airport's emergency medical staff reported that the man's pants and underwear were down around his ankles. And he had an immense smile on his face.

#

Bashir

B ASHIR HASSAN AL TIKRITI was arrested in Baghdad
on April 4, 2004 while delivering a tray of Turkish coffee
and pistachio honey cakes to a handful of mid-level clerks in
the Iraqi Ministry of Transportation.

Wrong place, wrong time.

Just as the young man was serving up the last finjan of
thick java, Moqtada al Sadr's Shi'a militia began shooting up
the place.

American helicopter gunships soon showed up and
began strafing and rocketing a nearby kindergarten and
maternity clinic, (" . . . with only minimal loss of life,"
according to the American Embassy).

Bashir took refuge behind an out-of-toner Ricoh copier
and was arrested when a squad of American Fifth Air Cavalry
stormed in.

Because he had a criminal record showing several minor
scrapes with the law—stealing tires, bunkering neft, smuggling
cigarettes—he was whisked away to Abu Ghraib Prison.
When his jailers discovered that Bashir was a Sunni *and* from
Tikrit, Saddam's hometown, the prisoner was re-classified
a 'high value' threat to humanity. Enhanced interrogation
techniques were applied. The means of persuasion included
water boarding, sleep deprivation, and the use of electricity
on the prisoner's scrotum.

Through the first several applications of liquid and
volts, Bashir told the truth—he was a pastry and coffee
delivery boy and didn't know *any*thing about *any*thing. His
remonstrations, however, failed to convince his captors. He
was, after all, from Saddam's birth town. Almost certainly
one of the family.

Finally, when assured that the torture would stop if he

simply confessed to *some*thing, Bashir cooked up a fairy tale that unfortunately caused several of his innocent neighbors to wind up floating in the Tigris.

Bashir's confession did *not,* however, get him closer to the prison's exit. Rather, it confirmed his guilt, and within a week, he was flown to Guantanamo Bay, Cuba, for an indefinite internment.

The young man's ACLU court appointed lawyer, Leonard Grossman, worked long and hard to garner a writ of habeas corpus to bring Bashir before a judge. But the combined efforts of the Bush/Obama/Trump administrations had successfully turned back the calendar to 1214, the year before Magna Carta pretty much guaranteed the right of an accused to get his/her day in court.

Unable to prise the writ from the authorities, Grossman did his best to make life easier for his client. In 2007, the lawyer was able to provide Bashir with a small laptop computer, one with very, *very* limited Internet capabilities. The prisoner was *not* able to use email, engage in social media, or receive the news. But he soon discovered that he *was* able to access a pair of fascinating sites—re-runs of *All My Children,* and Match.com.

After six months of watching three to four hours a day of the daytime soap, Bashir could manage conversational English. He felt ready to try his luck on the other website.

First of all, he needed a bio. He understood that he could not reveal that he was a 'high value jihadi,' a guest for the foreseeable future of the American military. He reworked his story, trying to keep the tone American-sounding. Taking inspiration from *All My Children,* Bashir invented a new identity—Billy Clyde Lucci, a thirty-five-year-old former wrangler turned soccer coach. He decided to describe himself to Match.com women as "detained, but wanting to mingle."

Bio now complete, a single, final obstacle still remained before he could launch himself into the world of available femmes: he needed a photo.

Although all of his fellow prisoners at Gitmo sported beards, Bashir shaved his off in order to look more appealing. This caused a minor stir among the other detainees, hard-line jihadis for whom facial hair was as sacred as their family names. Our hero claimed eczema and thus skirted the criticism.

Bashir's freshly shaven face also drew the attention of one of the American guards, who questioned the young man.

The prisoner fessed up. "I go Match dot com and must to look good to mingle."

The soldier, Anquan Demarias Brown, from Yonkers, saw no harm, took a snapshot of the Iraqi, and helped him upload it.

The photo was a winner. Bashir had inherited the best features of his very good looking parents. Tariq, his father, was tall, swarthy, with curly black ringlets and a perfect set of pearly teeth. Reina, the prisoner's mother, was even more of a knockout—a willowy Circassian with freckles, full lips, scalding blue eyes, and a set of charming dimples.

No surprise then that Bashir's uploaded photo drew two hundred and twenty-nine responses in the first hour!

The budding Casanova had underestimated both his own good looks and the lustfulness of the viewing public.

His first response was sent to Janice Jankowski, of Battle Creek, Michigan, who listed her job as "packer at Kellogg's."

"Dear Janice

I thanking you by your nise leter. Befor I rite more, I needs to say you I be prizner. I not shure when I free. Maybe yeer. Maybe too. I looking for woman to help me live by real world. Maybe you?
Sinsere,
Billy Clyde Lucci

When Ms. Jankowski quickly responded that she would gladly wait for him no matter how long he might remain behind bars, Bashir knew he was on to something.

He sent the same letter to Gloria Chang, a forty-year-old computer programmer for Google, in Palo Alto. When Ms. Chang also responded eagerly, Bashir wrote her a second letter and added a few pertinent details, taken right from *All My Children,* (Year 12).

Dear Gloria

I say you I in jale. But I not say wat is crime or where I be. I be in Sing Sing prizen in Nu york. My crime is kidnap. But I no do crime. I try to save my dawter which I adopt. I ready to do all for her.
Sinsere,
Billy Clyde Lucci

The prisoner's poignant story coupled with his movie star good looks set Match.com ablaze. Requests to mingle flooded in from the four corners of the planet. Women of every nationality, age, ethnicity, religion, color, size and shape declared themselves ready, willing, and able to spend the rest of their days with Billy Clyde.

After just two weeks on line, Bashir realized he had to narrow his correspondence to only those women living in the United States. The several thousand female respondents from Europe, Asia, and South America were left in the lurch.

Over the next few months, a continued winnowing brought the mingle-ables down to a manageable dozen. Their correspondence was heart-felt, touching, but ultimately unrequitable, since the Adonis was behind bars and likely to stay that way.

Fate (as if you didn't know) took a hand in late 2010. After years of tireless work on behalf of his client, attorney Grossman finally wrung a concession from the military—a transfer from Gitmo to the federal prison in Yankton, South Dakota. Bashir and three Afghani desperados were being transferred to America's heartland.

The South Dakota governor protested, claiming the jihadis might escape and begin terrorizing farm communities, maybe even set fire to the prairie.

His complaints fell on the Pentagon's deaf ears, and the four inmates were hustled onto a CIA Gulfstream and flown out of Cuba under bright blue, January skies. But as soon as their plane arrived over the mainland, the weather turned nasty. And by the time they hit the Midwest, a blizzard/white-out forced them to land in Sioux City, Iowa—sixty-some miles short of their goal.

The airfield being totally socked in for the foreseeable future, the men were taken off the plane and locked in a small hangar. A single guard stood vigil.

Claiming he needed to go number two, Bashir was unshackled and escorted to the pilots' changing room-cum-bathroom.

Left on his own, the prisoner rummaged through the lockers and quickly found a set of oil-stained overalls, a bomber jacket, a wool cap, and high boots. And a smart phone. And a fold-up map of the surroundings, a quick perusal of which showed that one of his Match.com soul mates was just a stone's throw away. He forced a window and disappeared into the storm.

Andrea DellaTorre, night clerk at the Sioux City Days Inn, was plagued with worry. The twenty-eight-year old divorcee felt crushed by her penurious life style. Would she ever get beyond her mind-numbing and poor-paying job? Would she ever be quit of her nagging ex-husband?

Andrea didn't want much, didn't need much. And at this stage, didn't hope for much.

Then her cell phone rang.

Bashir was waiting for her next to one of the cement pillars supporting US 129 as it cloverleafed overhead with US 29, about two miles north of Sioux Gateway Airport.

Despite his oil-smelly clothes and his snow encrusted head and hands, he appeared to Andrea even more gorgeous and desirable than his Match.com photo. Ready to mingle? God, she was so ready.

For his part, the escapee thought the woman in whose pickup he was now sitting was lovely beyond his wildest dreams, and certainly beyond the demure photo she had posted on-line.

Bashir saw a full-bosomed bombshell with long and curly blond hair that cascaded down her shoulders like a golden sunrise over the Euphrates. Her eyes were a startling green, like the oasis at Palmyra, and shone wild and eager.

The escapee and his abettress looked longingly at each other as they sat under the overpass.

"I now escape," he confessed.

"But isn't Sing Sing in New York?"

"Yes. They takes me to other prison. I see chance and leap."

"How did you find me?"

He showed her his newly purloined smart phone.

Andrea wasn't about to question his sub-standard English or her good fortune. She made a snap decision. "You'll need to hide. New clothes. New identification. You must be hungry." She started up her Ford Bronco.

"Where we go?" he asked.

"I can't take you home. Mother wouldn't understand. But don't worry, you'll be safe. I'll hide you." She reached over and clasped his hand. She almost swooned. So did he.

The jihadi's escape was only discovered ninety-six minutes after his jump from the hangar window. Some might attribute the long delay in discovering his absence to luck, karma, or b'shert. Perhaps kismet. Actually, federal ineptitude is a safer call. Seems that Sgt. Fernando Pimental, the single guard overseeing the four prisoners, had a history of sudden-onset grand mal seizures (an affliction he had successfully kept hidden from the Army). The combination of lack of sleep, most of a pint of Jack Daniels, and six lines of very good Columbian snort produced such a seizure five minutes after Pimental had locked Bashir in the bathroom. The guard was discovered only when one of the local pilots found him writhing on the hangar floor.

The FBI was immediately contacted but was reluctant to call a DEFCON 1, Code Red Alert, fearing it might cause a public panic.

They were overridden by the U.S. Attorney General. "Fuck the public," the AG was heard to shout. "We gotta find that Muslim piece o' shit before he drives a semi into a Christmas parade."

All stops were pulled and elements of the BATF, NSA, CIA, state police, national guard, and state militia joined the FBI in the hunt for Bashir Hassan al Tikriti.

When the news broke, a nosey reporter at the Omaha World-Herald searched for an angle. The next morning's headlines said it all: 'Saddam's nephew loose on the Great Plains!'

Needless to say, the FBI had been right. The panic that ensued brought to a screeching halt all but the most essential activities in a seven state region of the Mid-West. Schools closed, businesses shuttered for lack of customers, roadblocks prevented food shipments from going in or out of the blockaded region. Markets were denuded within hours as people hunkered down and barricaded themselves in their homes. Nine months later, maternity wards in every local hospital were over-booked.

But as desperately as the searchers searched, the escapee remained at large.

The last room on the second floor corridor of the Sioux City Days Inn had acquired over the years a musty-lived-in-tobacco stench that no amount of Good Housekeeping recommended cleaner (Lysol, maybe Pinesol) could even begin to disguise.

But for Bashir, it was heaven. After a long, hot bath, he and Andrea made plans for the remainder of the afternoon and the rest of their lives.

Because he was the same size as Josh, her ex, and because that louse had never quite moved out of her life, Andrea produced a ready supply of Jeans, shirts, under- and over- garments, and socks. She burned Bashir's prison togs in the motel's incinerator.

Although sex was foremost in each of their minds, both were shyly reluctant to take the first step.

Bashir sought to divert. "I to phone lawyer?" he asked Andrea.

"What're you thinkin', hon?" she replied.

Bashir was unsure what 'hon' meant, but let it slide. "If we to marry, I gets green card. Govermen can no to throw me."

"Good plan," she agreed, taking his hand and moving it onto her thigh.

Two days of fruitless searching for the escaped jihadi had brought the government's efforts to a fever pitch. Part of the problem for the G-Men lay in the fact that the cordon thrown around Sioux City had included only the main highways.

Born and raised in rural Iowa, Andrea knew that the farm-country back roads would lead them to safety. And thus, six days after his escape, he and Andrea were on the beach, soaking up the sun, and listening to the crashing Pacific.

Because Bashir was familiar with Whitey Bulger's story, (hiding in plain sight) he felt himself safe and quickly found work: barista in a Santa Monica, ocean-side Starbucks during the day, and bus boy at the Marmont Hotel on the

Sunset Strip during the night.

A month into his new life, he was spotted at the hotel by a Hollywood luminary who was looking for a 'type' to play an Iraqi Secret Policeman in *Argo*. Bashir auditioned and got the part.

And because nothing succeeds like success, he was scooped up for *Zero Dark Thirty*. (Bashir is one of UBL's guards and has three scenes fighting Navy Seal Team 6).

He was then hired for work on *American Sniper*. (Bashir is the second Arab shot by the sharpshooter).

All of these roles were small and uncredited, but sufficient for the escapee to earn his SAG card and move on to a featured role in *Homeland*.

America. You gotta love it.

Epilogue

Andrea and Bashir live in a small bungalow in Laurel Canyon. She works part-time at a famous Sunset Boulevard hotel's front desk. They are expecting twin girls.

When his infirmity was discovered, Sergeant Pimental was given an honorable discharge. He soon found a job at the Day's Inn in Sioux City, working the front desk.

Josh, Andrea's ex-husband has twice remarried and continues to make the lives of everyone he knows miserable.

Anquan Demarias Brown, the Gitmo guard who photographed Bashir and uploaded it to Match.com is running for Mayor of

Yonkers. He has successfully kept his role in the disappearance of Bashir Hassan al Tikriti deeply buried.

Leonard Grossman has left the poor-paying work at the ACLU and has gone corporate, signing on with Facebook's legal defense team.

Tariq and Reina al Tikriti are now living in a Beirut high-rise condo, the gift of their fairly well-to-do actor/son.

An English satirist and impersonator saw a fascinating story on Google, and began work immediately on a screenplay. He contacted SAG to help find someone who might provide technical assistance, and perhaps even star in the role. Check it out at: https://www.google.com/search?q=gitmo+match.com&ie=utf-8&client=firefox-b-1

#

The Lawsuit

I'M BEING SUED by my wife's current boyfriend. The reason for the legal action? A problem in the backyard of my home last Thursday. Actually, former home. I don't live there anymore since my wife, Muriel, insisted I leave two months ago. "Get the fuck outta here, you piece of shit," I believe were her exact words. I might not have heard correctly as I was busy ducking the small, potted aloe vera she had winged at me.

The boyfriend, Duke (really!), was apparently trying to start my chain saw. According to my daughter Sophie, who observed the entire event, he wanted to cut up some pallets for kindling.

Now, I've owned that tool for over twenty years and have learned a thing or two about running it. If you're going to be cutting in cold weather (ten above when 'the incident' occurred), you bring the chain saw *inside* several hours *before,* to warm it up.

According to Sophie, Duke didn't feel that was a necessary step. I'm guessing he had never worked a chain saw. See, Duke's a pharmacist. Scads of money. And if I know my soon to be ex-wife, he probably has a medicine cabinet crammed with opioids.

Anyhow, he retrieved the saw from the shed and began pulling on the cord. A dozen times, according to Sophie. No go. Nada. Cold motor. (Muriel, if you're wondering, was away, getting a facial).

Duke began overheating. Took off his down vest and woolen watch cap. Tried again. Choked it too much and flooded it. Sophie then suggested he remove the spark plug, pull the cord a couple times, then bring the machine inside and wait until the gas in the cylinder evaporated.

He looked at her (she reported) as if she were her father's smart-ass daughter, which, I am deeply proud to say, she is.

Ungraciously, Duke decided to take her advice. Fifteen minutes later he re-assembled the saw, returned to the backyard and had another go. Nothing the first nine pulls (Sophie was counting).

On the next pull, the engine turned over for a few seconds, then died. Duke, a big guy, was now seriously sweating. He took off his gloves, the ones that have those little grippy things on the fingers—designed specifically to help you hold on to your chain saw when you're trying to start it on a cold day.

Sophie thinks this was his big mistake, because on the next pull, things went horribly awry.

The machine caught with a roar, and since Duke had failed to engage the brake, the chain began spinning around the bar at Mach 3. And because he wasn't wearing gloves, the cutting instrument slipped from his sweaty hands and fell, nose first, directly onto his right foot.

I think I failed to mention that Duke was wearing flip-flops. With gym socks, of course. After all, it *was* ten above.

Those socks, ultimately, served a very useful purpose. True, they in no way impeded the saw's needle sharp teeth from slicing into Duke's right foot, from the big toe, across the top of his metatarsals, coming to a end just below the lateral malleolus (that big, bony thing on the outside of your ankle).

The socks came into play immediately as a super absorbent dressing that soaked up some of the torrents of blood that began spewing out of Duke's foot and darkening the snow in all directions.

Luckily for him, Sophie is a trained EMT. She knew what to do and did it—staunched the bleeding, then called 911.

Since both Duke and Sophie were in the ER when Muriel came home with her new face, there was no one to explain to her the blood-red snow around the woodshed. For some inexplicable reason, she phoned me (the "piece of shit") and demanded to know what I had done to Duke and why it looked like Stalingrad in the backyard. I was mystified and pled innocent.

Muriel then called Sophie, learned the awful truth, and rushed to the hospital.

So did Muriel's lawyer, Jacob Nussbaum. The attorney assured the careless woodsman that I had obviously not maintained the chain saw in proper working order, and thus, I would be liable for the several hundred thousand dollars it would take to graft a new big toe onto Duke's foot. Add to that a couple hundred grand for pain, suffering and lost wages and we were suddenly talking real money.

Happily, Sophie, my angel girl, has given a complete report to the police and to the doctors. *My* lawyer assures me the judge will throw out their case as frivolous—a waste of the court's time. He says I can then countersue.

Sophie has been accepted to NYU for pre-med. I'm pretty sure I've found her the money.

#

Original Sin

THE ROMAN WINTER had been particularly harsh. The last time the Tiber had frozen over was more than sixty years earlier, in 1030. The extended cold snap allowed the peat and firewood merchants to prosper, even as their supplies dwindled.

The poor of Rome, naturally, suffered miserably and had the added misfortune of being caught up in a short but virulent typhoid epidemic that left thousands of children dead.

Pope Urban II, fully cognizant of his place of primacy in Christendom and of his supreme importance to his far-flung flock, kept himself safe, warm, and sequestered in the Castel Sant'Angelo. He had ordered only the most important rooms in the Tiber-side fortress to be heated.

One of those rooms, the Pope's cozy, private library, was now being prepared for a hastily called meeting. Foot warmers had been placed in front of cushioned chairs arranged around a fireplace crackling with a cheery pile of burning logs. Woolen blankets were stacked nearby. Pewter carafes of mulled wine and hot cider were at hand to accompany the light meal being kept warm on the sideboard.

Luigi Albanese, the Pope's aged secretary, was sharpening quills just as three red-robed cardinals entered. Two went immediately to the fire to warm themselves. The third crossed directly to the food.

"His Holiness is delayed, Your Eminences," the secretary explained, with not quite the deference in his tone the three cardinals were used to. "His Holiness requests that you not wait for him," Albanese continued, gesturing to the food and drink.

"Many thanks to you, Luigi," said Cardinal Lorenzo

Caprivi, spooning a pair of fried eggs and a slab of ham onto a gold leaf plate. The good-looking, swarthy, twenty-five-year old Neapolitan was among the youngest in the Vatican's College of Cardinals. Caprivi had not been a partisan of the new pope when Urban succeeded the short-lived Victor III, in 1087. Urban suspected as much, but recognized in Caprivi just the kind of man he wanted close at hand: clever, straight talking, and utterly ruthless when it came to the enemies of Mother Church. That the cardinal from Naples kept company with the best looking altar boys in the Vatican was *"no one's business but his own,"* Urban was heard to remark.

"I hear His Holiness has received a letter from the East," Caprivi probed delicately through a mouthful of egg. He raised his eyebrows speculatively. "Are the Byzantines up to something?"

The secretary stared at the cardinal with a blank expression. "Your Eminence, I would know nothing of that," Albanese answered.

The cardinal accepted the secretary's comments at face value, understanding full well that *nothing* in the entire Pontificate happened without the knowledge of Luigi Albanese. No incident of whoring bishop or drunken priest escaped his notice. Let an over-eager cleric acquire too many benefices, Albanese was in the know. And when the Catharians in French Languedoc began to doubt the centrality of the Crucifixion, Albanese had his spies and agents in place to uncover the heretics and mete out the appropriate punishment.

"Byzantium! Fah," said Cardinal Mario Morandi, spitting an olive pit into his one good hand. The razor thin man had lost the other in battle in 1084, during the Sack of Rome by the barbarian Normans. Morandi and a dozen other priests had barricaded themselves into a Benedictine monastery near Rome's port of Ostia. The Normans put the building to the torch, but Morandi organized a spirited defense and the invaders were repulsed. In the end, he was elevated to bishop, then archbishop, and six years later donned the cardinal's red cassock and hat.

Morandi now helped himself to a generous portion of prosciutto and goat cheese. "Those Byzantine pseudo-Christians can go straight to hell. Every last one of them." He gulped down half a goblet of wine. "Eastern Rite, my ass. Jesu save me from those apostate bastards."

"Absolutely right, Mario," added Cardinal Gennaro Ricci, standing in front of the fireplace and warming his ample backside. The triple jowled Ricci, still favoring the tonsured pate of his former mendicant order, was perhaps the College's most ambitious cardinal and had lobbied mightily for his own accession to the Papacy in open competition with Urban. But when Ricci was found to have fathered twin girls, his candidacy lost momentum. Although his parenting performance was not unique among the Vatican's supposed celibates, Ricci's dalliance had special circumstances that proved unconscionable, even for the thick skinned-cardinals: the mother of the twins was Ricci's own half-sister, Beatrice.

"If it's a letter from Constantinople," Ricci now suggested, "you can wager Patriarch Alexios didn't write it. His Latin is laughable. He still thinks *'caveat emptor'* was the warning given to Caesar on his way to the forum."

The joke, an old one, drew sniggers from the other two cardinals and a small smile from the secretary.

A sudden brisk rapping at the library's door interrupted the moment.

"Come," ordered the Pope's secretary.

The door cracked open and a young orderly popped his head in. "His Holiness, the Pope, is on the way," he announced, stepping back from the portal.

Within half a minute, Urban II, a florid-faced, short and portly man of fifty-three with an unruly spray of gray hair bustled into the room. He was dressed in a floor length heavy ermine coat and a thick red wool scarf. He carried a scrolled parchment under one arm.

"Gentlemen," the Pope began. "Thank you for coming on such short notice. And in such God-awful weather. Jesu! When will it warm up?" Urban turned to Morandi. "How's your gout, sir? Cold playing havoc with your knee, I dare say."

Cardinal Morandi was frankly surprised that Urban knew of his medical condition, an affliction he had attempted to keep *sub rosa*. He looked at Caprivi briefly, who nodded in the direction of the Pope's secretary, still busying himself with his quill sharpening. Morandi understood at once. "Your Holiness," the cardinal said, "with God's grace, I'll survive to see the flowers bloom again along the Tiber."

"I pray it be so," Urban said, handing the scroll to Caprivi. "A letter of the utmost urgency. From Patriarch Alexios, in Byzantium. If you please, Cardinal."

Caprivi took the scroll and advanced to stand near the fire while the holy men settled themselves into the chairs, feet aimed at the fireplace. They tucked blankets around their laps.

Caprivi quickly scanned the parchment and began, "From His Most Exalted, Alexios I, the Arch Patriarch of Constanti. . . "

"Skip that part and get to the point," commanded the Pope, testily.

"As you wish, Your Holiness," Caprivi answered, bowing slightly. "Alexios writes: 'Dearest Urban, our Cousin in Christ: We Christians in the East are being besieged by ravening hoards of Mussulmen Turks, infidel non-believers who profess fealty to their god, someone called 'Allah.' The Byzantine Empire's outlying towns are being savaged. The very gates of Constantinople will soon be threatened if you do not come to our immediate assistance. Please, in Christ's name, help us. Your brother, Alexios.'"

"First he's your cousin, then he's your brother. Which is it?" asked Cardinal Morandi, his voice dripping with undisguised scorn.

"He is neither, thank God," said Cardinal Ricci, sucking the marrow out of a beef bone. "This is not *our* problem. The Turks are not threatening Rome. Let the Byzantines tend to their own fields." Ricci licked his fingers and wiped them on a woolen blanket.

Caprivi carefully rolled up the scroll and placed it back on the table. He held up a hand to Ricci. "Patience, gentlemen. Patience." He turned to Pope Urban and began slowly. "Perhaps, Your Holiness, this is the opening we've long sought. A chance to bring the heretical easterners back under the control of the One, True Mother Church. Think how this opportunity might increase papal influence *and* papal coffers."

Pope Urban bent forward, clearly intrigued by the direction the cardinal seemed to be going. He didn't trust Caprivi for a moment—there was no such thing as a Cardinal who did not see himself Pope—but the man was as cunning as any Neapolitan ever born and had great political instincts. "Go on, Cardinal Caprivi. You have my attention."

But before Caprivi could continue, Ricci interrupted.

"Of course there is an *'opportunity'* here, Caprivi," Ricci said in his thick Romagnole accent. "But please, gentlemen, let's not lose sight of the fact that we are barred by Canon Law from entering into a war simply to satisfy a *political* or *financial* agenda. Remember the early church fathers' theory on the *'Just War.'* "

Caprivi looked skyward, wondering to himself how this fool had become elevated to one of the most exalted posts in all of Christendom. "We've tweaked that theory for years, Gennaro," said Caprivi with more patience than the man deserved. "This is neither the time . . . and certainly not the place," his outstretched hand swept across the Papal library, "to quibble about Canon Law."

"I completely agree," said the Pope, impatience coloring his voice. "Let's not split hairs about who can or who cannot make war. Times have changed, Cardinal Ricci. Wouldn't you agree?"

Abashed, Ricci bowed his head. "Of course, Your Holiness. I should not have assumed that Canon Law need be consulted, and it was presumptuous of me to believe it had any relevance here in your private library."

"Thank you for your support, cardinal. It is a wise man who acknowledges his mistakes."

"I completely agree with Your Holiness," said Morandi, getting up and tossing a small, knotty oak stump onto the fire. He used an iron poker to arrange the log on the andirons. "But please, gentlemen, consider these two substantial obstacles. Such a military mission to support Byzantium would entail the raising of a huge army. Where do we get the money and the men?"

Ricci jumped back in, anxious to regain Pope Urban's

pleasure and trust. "Money? The usual place . . . from the sale of indulgences. Let the peasants pay for the war and at the same time buy their way into heaven. It's worked before."

"All well and good," Morandi conceded, leaning the poker against the stone fireplace. "But what about the army?"

"The army? Again no problem," said Ricci, raising his bulky body from his chair and joining Morandi in front of the fireplace. "We'll sell a holy war. We get the soldiers to wear crucifixes on their armor. We'll call it . . . " He searched for the proper phrase. "We'll call it . . . the *War of the Cross*. If they fall in battle, they get to sit at the right hand of the Prince of Peace. It's a perfect recruiting tool."

The Pope nodded appreciatively. "Yes, Ricci. Wonderful idea. I like that one very much."

Back in Papal favor, Ricci beamed.

"Very well," said Morandi. "That takes care of the costs and the army. But there are still two points you overlook, Gennaro. You said a 'holy war.' Number one: what's holy about this war? And number two: how do we justify sending out an army of Christians with a Papal mandate to kill? It's at odds with the 6th Commandment. I hope you all remember that one: *Thou shalt not kill*. A war like this could bring unneeded censure on our heads and give strength to the heretics. The last thing we need."

The holy men fell silent. After a minute, Caprivi spoke. "Let's try this," he said, measuring his words carefully. "We can make the war holy by *expanding* it."

Urban looked on with growing interest. "What are you thinking, cardinal? Expand? How?"

Caprivi took his time and walked to the food. He ladled

a small bowl of steaming onion soup into a beautifully carved wooden bowl. He carefully sipped at the soup, smacking his lips. He turned again toward the three men. "These Mussulmen control Jerusalem, correct? Let's motivate the troops with a holy mission whose purpose is to free Jerusalem from the infidels. Is that *holy* enough for you, Mario?"

"I like it," said Morandi. "Very much, in fact. We relieve Byzantium, coerce them back onto the path of the True Faith, *and* take control of the Holy Land. It's a neat package, gentlemen." With his good hand, Morandi stroked his well-trimmed beard. "But let's not call it a '*mission*.' Let's call it . . . " He paused to make sure he had everyone's attention. "Let's call it . . . *a crusade!*"

Urban clapped his hands. "Oh, brilliant, Morandi. Absolutely brilliant." He waved a hand through the air, as if reading a divine message writ on high. *'A crusade to free Jerusalem from the infidels.'* Read that back to me, Luigi."

The secretary cleared his throat: *'A crusade to free Jerusalem from the infidels,'* he intoned, stifling a yawn.

"Wait a moment," interjected Caprivi. "True, Jerusalem *is* governed by infidels. And, yes, it would provide excellent cover for our efforts to re-take Byzantium, but . . . " he trailed off.

"Why your hesitation, cardinal?" the Pope asked.

"Your Holiness. It seems that pilgrims to Jerusalem who have recently returned to Rome have all reported the same thing: that they were treated with *exceeding* kindness by those who now control the city. It will be difficult to arouse anti-Mussulman sentiment under those circumstances."

"Not at all, Caprivi," Ricci quickly responded. "I'll use my Office of the Holy See to make sure that rumors are circulated throughout all of Christendom telling of the brutal torture and murder of scores of saintly and peaceful Christian pilgrims. The *illiterati* are easily swayed."

The Pope nodded, smiling. "Yes, I agree, Cardinal Ricci. The great unwashed really *are* putty. But there's still the problem with the Sixth Commandment," he reminded the others.

The men fell silent, each wondering how their newly conceived army might function in the face of the admonition 'not to kill.'

"Your Holiness. If I might speak," said the secretary quietly.

"Please, Luigi."

Albanese put down his quill and came out from behind his desk. He bowed respectfully to the three Cardinals. He knew he was speaking out of turn, but he also understood that he had the Pope's protection. Standing before the four holy men, Albanese began slowly.

"As you may know, Your Holiness, Your Eminences, I've always believed in a much stricter interpretation of the Ten Commandments, especially the Sixth. The Commandments may have been given to *'the chosen people.'*" Here the secretary chuckled derisively. "But the commandments were really meant, as we all know, for use by the followers of Jesus, by any and all who call themselves Christians. We here in the Vatican understand that the intent of the Commandments is to guide the action of *Christians toward each other.* Mussulmen are *not* Christians, Your Holiness. Therefore, they do *not* fall under the protection of the Sixth Commandment and thus, they can be legally killed. *Quod erat demonstrandum*," he concluded.

The holy men looked at each other as if in the presence of The Revealed Truth.

"Q.E.D. indeed, Luigi. Bravo," the Pope declared, getting to his feet. "My friends. Problem solved," he said, briskly rubbing his hands together. "I'll preach *'a crusade to free Jerusalem from the infidels.'* It has a ring to it. Wouldn't you agree?"

The three Cardinals nodded vigorously, warming to the new project.

Pope Urban picked up a flagon of mulled wine and drank deeply, dribbling some onto his ermine robe. "I'd like to get started on this as soon as possible. Luigi, where do you suggest I go to preach this new war . . . er, crusade?"

As usual, the Pope's secretary was miles ahead of his master and the other holy men. He had already settled on the exact place he knew the Pope would agree to. "Might I suggest Clermont, your Holiness? The French king, Philip, is at present an excommunicant and would be most grateful if you were to lift that burden. In return, I'm certain he would revel in such a call to arms and would be able to provide untold men and money."

"Perfect, Luigi. Perfect," said the Pope. "Send word to Philip and to all of Christendom. Let's make it for early next winter. I'll go to Clermont for a general conclave."

The Pope then turned a cautionary look toward the holy men. "Gentlemen," he warned, "this meeting never took place. And Luigi, one more thing. Mark your notes 'For Papal Eyes Only' and bury them in the Vatican archives."

#

To an Isle in the Water . . .

PADDY DONNELLY WAS an eavesdropper. And today, wedged into a far corner of Sal and Jerry's Real Deli on West 86th, he was nosing into the half dozen within-earshot conversations that were providing fodder for '*Lost on Neptune,*' the second of his inter-planetary play writing trilogy.

Paddy especially favored Sal and Jerry's because the tables were almost on top of each other, making it so much easier to pick up slivers-of-life conversations. But more importantly, he came for a certain waitress who for months he'd been fancying from afar. He'd stare longingly at her, rapt, as she gracefully and effortlessly glided through the crowded restaurant. *She's taken ballet,* he jotted on his writing pad. Her movements reminded him of some long-forgotten poem. He wrote down as much of it as he could recall: *She carries in the dishes and . . .* and what? He couldn't dredge up the remaining lines. Dylan Thomas, he guessed. Maybe Yeats.

Though he could hardly take his eyes off of her, he knew he had to rein in his enthusiasm lest he repeat the catastrophe that surrounded the last time he was at the deli, two weeks earlier. His attention then had been so riveted on the young woman that he had drifted dreamily out of the restaurant, unaware that he had left behind two full writing tablets with weeks of notes, a detailed outline for the third *'Lost'* play (*Pluto*), full biographies of his new characters, and pencil sketches of his favorite waitress, including a long, rhapsodic description of her. In a frenzy, he had shown up at the restaurant early the next morning for an unsuccessful search. He promised himself that today he'd stay on task, especially since the jammed deli was offering barrels-full of literary grist.

Being a garrulous and affable young man, Paddy often made unsolicited recommendations to undecided patrons. "The pastrami here is so-so, but the corned beef can't be beat," he had sagely advised the well-dressed, older couple to his right, Lisbet and Anthony. They followed his advice and split a corned beef on rye with paper thin Swiss. Later, Anthony thanked Paddy, saying it was probably the best sandwich he had eaten in years. His wife agreed.

The couple had hardly left their table before Paddy was hastily scribbling down a pungent quote Anthony had delivered, "*It's not my New York anymore,*" he had said, ruefully. *"Someone took it from me when I wasn't looking."*

Paddy double-underlined the quote on his pad. Then, seized with the kind of inspiration he found only at Sal and Jerry's, he crossed out *New York* and penciled in *Neptune.* He decided to put Anthony's amended quote in the mouth of Liam O'Hara, protagonist of the tri-partite space opera, captain of the intergalactic battle cruiser, *Shamrock II*, and sworn enemy of the brutish space pirate, Seamus Flynn.

With Lisbet and Anthony departed, Paddy now turned his attention to the small table on his left where three women were speaking in European-accented English. They were discussing an upcoming women's tennis event, a sport about which he knew almost nothing. He *did* have a dim childhood memory of once watching Wimbledon on his home tele in Cork, in the late 1990s. He vaguely recalled some kind of a paddle, a net, and players chasing a white ball. One of the sillier spectacles he had ever witnessed, he told people for years.

As the women were busily talking about lobs and sliced serves—whatever they were—the waitress, *his waitress*, came to refill their ice water.

Paddy left off from his writing and regarded her with barely concealed wonder. She was a slim, wisp of an attractive woman of about thirty with long auburn hair pulled back into a French-braided, thick-ropey ponytail that reached down between her shoulder blades. In the now-lost writing tablets, he had noted *'the perfect shape of her eyebrows, the radiance of her blue, luminous, almond-shaped eyes, set deeply over high, peachy-skinned and lightly freckled cheekbones.'*

As the waitress poured the refills, she caught a snatch of the women's conversation about tennis and jumped right in. Paddy listened as the four of them, now thick as thieves and all talking with great animation, discussed this sporting *terra incognita.*

Paddy looked up from his note taking just as the waitress took a purposeful step back from the women's table, got into what he imagined was a tennis-y pose, raised her right arm high above her head, paused a moment, then swung her arm down with force, simultaneously pronouncing "sharapova." The three women laughed with delight and nodded their approval. Paddy deduced that a sharapova must be some kind of Russian tennis maneuver, perhaps a heavy paddle blow. He wrote a quick note: *'Liam at Space Acad. self defense class. learns sharapova. uses in hand to hand w/Seamus. Google sharapova tonite.'*

With her refilling done at the one table, the waitress now stepped over to Paddy's.

The forgotten lines of poetry came back to him in a rush. *"She carries in the dishes, and lays them in row."* Yeats. But weren't there a few more lines?

He looked up at her, beaming. "You like tennis. I could

tell."

"My favorite sport," she answered with enthusiasm, reaching for his glass.

"I don't play myself, but I'm a big fan."

"Really? Been to Ashe for the Open?"

A vision of quicksand suddenly washed across Paddy's brain. *Ash for the open?* he repeated to himself. *Something's burned down, outside? In an open field, perhaps? No. No. That's not it. Maybe a place. That must be it. A place.*

"Nooo," he began nervously, watching her to see if he was on the right track. "But . . . when I was eight, my folks took me to the All Ireland Tennis Championships in Dublin."

"Interesting," she said. "I didn't know tennis was that big in Ireland. Who'd you see play?"

The pit of quicksand now took on a definite shape and began calling out to him. He heard her question as if it had been asked from miles away and the sound was reaching his ears in shorter and shorter bytes: *"Who did you see play? . . . did you see play? . . . you see play? . . . see play?"*

After a throaty swallow he hoped had gone unnoticed, he wheezed, "Saw Liam O'Hara. All-Irish champion right through the 90s." Paddy held his breath and looked straight into the waitress' brilliant blue eyes, then added, "Great champion, Liam. Very fluid. Ran like a deer, he did."

The waitress nodded a few times. "Liam O'Hara? Why do I know that name?" she said carefully, with a look on her face that showed Paddy she was sorting through her smart phone's contact list.

The quicksand now reached up to his thighs. *"Keep it up you bloody idjit. Another minute you'll be swimmin' in it."*

He watched her beautifully wrinkled brow suddenly

smooth. *She's found Liam,* he screamed internally. *But how could she? He doesn't exist.*

The waitress continued to regard him without blinking, the hint of an all-knowing smile playing on the corners of her mouth. "Who did Liam play?" she asked slowly, as if she already knew the answer.

Stick a fork in me. I'm done, Paddy thought, the quicksand now up to his neck. "Who . . . who did Liam play?" he croaked. He looked down at his pad for a moment, then slowly raised his head. "Seamus," Paddy squeaked. "Flynn. Seamus Flynn. Liam played Seamus Flynn."

The waitress nodded. "I thought so," she said.

Paddy knew he should have shut up then and there and ordered a large hemlock. Instead, he slugged on, his mouth seemingly with a life of its own—divorced from brain, reason, rationality.

"But Seamus was too old for Liam," Paddy offered gamely. Then, summoning a sly smile, he added what he imagined was proof of his tennis expertise. "Seamus couldn't manage the sharapovas as well as Liam," he pronounced decisively.

The waitress was now smiling broadly, seemingly enjoying the torture. "They *are* difficult," she agreed, then asked, "Straight sets?"

Straight sets? Curved sets? Curly sets? Paddy thought wildly, his eyes bugging, his bowels audibly gurgling. "Definitely," he finally got out. "The champ loved straight sets. Wouldn't have it any other way."

The waitress gave him a smile he supposed an indulgent parent might bestow on a tale-telling child caught up in an easily-seen-through fib. "Gotta go," she said lightly, raising her hand above her head and bringing it gently down. "Those sharapovas. Tricky," she added, turning away.

Paddy put both elbows on the table and cupped his face in his palms. *You bloody effing moron. What is it about your mouth? Why can't you control it?* He took a deep breath and peeked through his fingers. The waitress was mercifully gone.

To his left, the three women were winding up. He surveyed their plates and noticed that two of them had done justice to their lunches. The third had grievously over-ordered. Paddy turned to his writing tablets and quickly reviewed what he had written about them.

The first woman, facing Paddy, he had described as *'a tall, dusty-blond w/dark eyes, pretty, rounded tanned face.' @ 40, dressed white/black Spandex.* He thought he heard her addressed as "Maria." She had ordered a cup of matzo ball soup and a Chinese chicken salad. She finished the soup and left only a very small piece of bok choy on her plate. *'Maria made short work of meal,'* Paddy had jotted down. Now he appended an afterthought: *'As if Cromwell's Roundheads were breathing down her neck.'* He re-read this last sentence and immediately scratched it out. *Way too obscure.*

The second woman, sitting down the wall from Paddy, whose name sounded like a hyphenated-garble of too many foreign consonants, was *'younger, light complected w/ thinning, brownish hair, gray eyes, no chin & large teeth.' Dressed striped red/white shorts and solid red, long sleeved blouse.* The woman had sneezed twenty-two times during her meal. After the fourth one, he'd counted. But despite her obvious infirmity, she'd worked her way nicely through a Caesar salad and a large bowl of fresh fruit.

The third woman, called Tania, was sitting next to Paddy on his immediate left, not more than two feet from his elbow. He wrote, *'unusually thin, almost emaciated.'* v*ery pale, w/short, spiky dark hair, wearing blue, sleeveless, boat-collar blouse that called attn to bone-thin neck/arms.* Paddy thought she had made a valiant attempt at lunch, but not near good enough. *'Tania started w/ bowl, <u>not cup</u>, beef/barley. finished, using 2 slices rye to clean bowl.'*

The soup had been followed by a breast of smoked turkey sandwich on whole wheat with cranberries and potato salad on the side. It had been delivered, cut into quarters, on a huge oval platter. As soon as it was put in front of Tania, Paddy wrote, *'No way T can finish. Not even with help of friends, Maria and ????'*

Tania had taken her time and had worked her way deliberately through one quarter of the sandwich. She'd eaten with determination, and Paddy had rooted for her. But *'after taking only 2 reluctant bites of 2nd 1/4, T put sand. down - pushed plate away.'*

Seeing that her customers had finished eating, the waitress returned. She glanced toward Paddy. "Seamus," she smiled at him. "Too old for Liam."

There was nothing he could do but blush. "Far too old," he agreed, apologizing with a shrug, a goofy grin, and raised eyebrows.

She shook her head with a kindly laugh, turned to the women, and tallied their checks. Tania asked about wrapping up the turkey sandwich.

"Be happy to," said the waitress. She took a single credit card—Maria was springing for lunch—gathered up the women's dishes and made her way serenely back to the kitchen.

She's definitely studied ballet, Paddy thought. He now recalled that during their discussion of tennis, the women and the waitress had used the word *'tak'*. Paddy had heard Russians use this word and, remembering the sharapova paddle smash, concluded that the four women must be Russian speakers.

When the waitress returned a few minutes later with credit card and doggie bag, Paddy signaled to her that he, too, would like a check. She moved over a step and began totaling his bill. "Enjoy your meal?" she asked.

"Wonderful, as usual. I'm a regular."

She looked up from her writing. "I know you are. I've seen you here a few times," she said matter-of-factly, holding his gaze. "But not for a couple of weeks. Been hiding?" she asked playfully.

She remembered him! He could hardly believe it. Now he had to respond. And quickly. But what to say? That he recalled her, too? That he always tried to sit in her section? That he thought her fabulous, graceful, lovely-to-behold? That he would never, ever lie to her again? That he was very much wanting a permanent relationship and was she, perhaps, available?

"You're Russian, aren't you?" was the best he could do.

"Yes," she said, brightly. "I didn't know my accent was still so strong."

"I heard you and the ladies say *'tak,'* and I guessed. My name's Patrick, but my friends call me Paddy."

She paused a moment before answering, "My name's Natasha." Another pause. "My friends call me Natasha," she deadpanned, raising one eyebrow archly. Then she smiled to soften her gentle jest at his expense.

The joke was on him, he realized, and he found the experience exhilarating. If this woman wanted to tease him from here to next Tuesday, he was ready to be teased.

Up until then, Paddy had only noticed the *accent* in Natasha's speech. Now he became fully aware of the *quality* of her voice. It wasn't sweet-sounding. It wasn't melodious. It had, rather, a deep, throaty, almost grating cast to it. But when she said her name, "Natasha," with an Old World inflection, he felt as if he were wrapped in an eiderdown on a windy winter's evening.

"I'm in America about five years," she said, softly.

Feeling totally forgiven for his tennis tall tales, Paddy could not stop smiling. He realized it was his turn again to speak. He considered telling her that he, too, was a recent immigrant, fifteen years earlier from Ireland. Instead, he acted on a sudden impulse. "Listen. I've just finished reading a wonderful novel. One I think you'd really enjoy." He hurriedly pulled a well-worn paperback from the pocket of his windbreaker. "It's about immigrants to America and I absolutely loved it. It's called *O Pioneers*." He handed it to her.

Natasha put down the stack of dishes she had started to collect, wiped her hands carefully on her apron, took the book, and began reading the synopsis on the back cover.

"You can have it. A gift," he said.

Her answer was a gracious and shyly sweet smile. "I'd love to read it," she said, her voice becoming even quieter as she inclined her head in a gesture of thanks. In that briefest of moments, Paddy was able to glimpse the nape of her neck. He saw a small tangle of fiery red-brown hair that had refused to be corralled into her ponytail. It seemed to him a secret place, one that beckoned to him with a promise of delicious danger.

A short silence followed. Neither rushed to fill it. Natasha slid the book into her apron pocket and once more took up Paddy's dishes. "Thanks again," she said, almost whispering now, and turned toward the kitchen.

A bawling infant two tables away brought him back to real time. He looked at his check, saw it was for just over sixteen dollars, took out his wallet, and placed a twenty in clear view. Then added a five.

While he and Natasha had been talking, the three next-table women had left. But the doggie bag, Paddy noticed at once, remained exactly where Natasha had placed it.

He picked up his pad and wrote: *'Did T forget it or decide not to take it?'*

Paddy retrieved his knapsack from under the table, put it on his lap, opened it up wide and carefully packed his two writing tablets. He looked around the deli and then quickly and expertly scooped the doggie bag into the knapsack, rose, squeezed out from behind his table, and headed for the front of the restaurant.

He had almost reached the door when Tania, the sandwich's owner, re-entered. They recognized each other at once. Paddy stepped back to let her pass.

"I forgot my lunch," she explained breathlessly, brushing by him and heading toward the back of the deli.

Paddy exited the restaurant, rapidly covered the several dozen paces to the 86th Street subway, and hustled down the stairs.

In the kitchen, Natasha leafed through her new gift. Her attention was caught by Willa Cather's description of the American heartland, *"There are always dreamers on the frontier,"* the author had written. Natasha dog-eared the page and continued thumbing through the novel. Between pages sixteen and seventeen, she found a scrap of folded newspaper. As she began to unfold it, a sudden commotion in the restaurant brought her to the kitchen doors. She popped one ajar. At the back of the deli, one of the women who had just left was ranting to a waitress. Natasha placed the book in her apron and made her way toward the uproar.

"Where's my damn sandwich?" the woman fumed, attracting the attention of the few remaining lunch customers. "I bet *he* took it."

"Who?" asked the other waitress.

"The tall, red headed guy with the orange beard and the million freckles. He was sitting right next to me," she said. "The guy *you* were talking to when we left," Tania said, pointing an accusing finger at Natasha.

"I don't know anything about it," Natasha said.

Alerted by the shouting, Jerry Sternweiss, the eighty-four-year-old owner of Sal and Jerry's, shuffled over.

"Nu? Vus machs da?" he demanded.

Although not a Yiddish speaker, Natasha divined her boss' question and explained the situation to him.

"Not to worry young lady," Jerry said to Tania, placing an ancient hand gently on her thin shoulder. He turned to the other waitress. "Go make this fine young woman a replacement sandwich and send her home happy."

Mollified, Tania calmed down and accompanied the other waitress to the front counter. Jerry trailed slowly after them.

Natasha watched them briefly, wondering about her million-freckled Irishman. She took out *O Pioneers,* found the newspaper scrap, and read the very short article by the paper's theater critic.

New Play at the Jamison
by Artemis Sarfondis

Lost on Jupiter, the new three act play by writer Patrick Donnelly was as awful a piece of play writing as this reviewer has ever had the misfortune to witness. Trite, inane, jejune, sophomoric—and those are just for openers. For fifty-five excruciating minutes this reviewer prayed for lightening to strike the author, and if not kill him outright, at least afflict him with palsy so that his promised sequel, *Lost on Neptune,* might never see the light of day.

Natasha's heart went out to Paddy. *Poor dear boy,* she thought. But at least she now had a last name to go with the missing doggie bag. If Patrick Donnelly had, in fact, taken it.

"So. You're telling me he's mostly red-orange? Is that it? Curly red hair? Curlier red beard? Rosy freckles? *Orangish* eyebrows? I'm not sure I've ever seen anyone colored quite like that," Charlotte said, taking the cozy off the tea pot and pouring two steaming cups of Russian Caravan.

Natasha reached out to a plate on which a pair of apple Danish—borrowed from Sal and Jerry's —were waiting to be eaten. "He also has the most beautiful voice, Char. This very soft Irish accent. But not a tenor. It's deeper."

"Baritone, sounds like," Charlotte suggested, dropping a pair of sugar cubes into her china cup. "Okay. So now we're all in a dither about a red-haired, red-faced *baritone.* Marvelous. Are you going to see him again?"

"I'm not sure. I don't know where to find him. I think he stole someone's doggie bag."

Charlotte put down her cup in mid-sip. "Well that's just great! A red-haired, red freckled-faced baritone who's also a thief."

"I can hardly fault him for stealing food," Natasha said, pointing with her fork to their purloined dessert.

"Right. Let he who is without sin . . . etcetera," Charlotte said, slicing the cheese Danish neatly into quarters. "What else do you know about him?"

"Have a look at these," Natasha said, taking two yellow tablets out of the table drawer. "His writing pads. He's a playwright. He left these in the deli a couple weeks ago. Look at this Char, he writes about me. And here," Natasha said, showing Paddy's sketches. "He's even drawn me."

Charlotte spent a few minutes leafing through the tablets. "Uh huh. He's either severely smitten or he's a stalker."

"He's no stalker, Char. He seriously likes me. I can tell."

"And how 'bout you?"

Natasha ran her fingers through her long hair, then hugged her bathrobe tightly around herself. "I like him, too. He has this . . . sweetness."

"So go find him. It's your day off. Should only take a year or two to track him down. I mean, there's only twelve million people in what we jokingly refer to as 'greater Manhattan.' How many Paddy . . . what's his last name . . . can there be in New York City?"

"Donnelly. Patrick Donnelly."

"Am I the biggest twit on the planet, Jimmy? Be honest with me."

James Feeny, bartender at *Tibor's Old Budapest* in central Brooklyn, roommate and confidant to his best friend, Paddy Donnelly, stood behind the restaurant's bar, cleaning glasses. "From all you've told me, Paddy darlin', you certainly would seem to rank up there. And if not the *biggest* twit on the planet, then surely top five."

Paddy slouched over the bar and took a small sip from the bottle of tonic water he'd been nursing since coming on duty at *Tibor's,* an hour earlier. "She actually remembered me, Jimmy. From other times I'd been at the deli. She asked where I'd been hiding. Does that mean she's missed seeing me?" Paddy shook his head. "As if I could hide anything from her. Especially after that tennis malarkey. What was I thinking? She saw through me in an instant. Anyone else would have told me—and properly so—to bugger off. But she didn't seem bothered that I'm a total airhead. I tell you, Jim, I think she fancies me. Is it possible?"

"'Course it's possible. Twit and all, Paddy, you're a catch and every woman who comes here to the restaurant knows it. 'Cept for Maureen, the evil witch of the north. You are so better off rid of her."

Paddy smiled up at his friend, taking heart. "So, Jim. A plan. That's what I need."

After Charlotte left for work, Natasha poured another cup of tea, opened *O Pioneers,* and re-read the newspaper review of '*Lost on Jupiter.*' "Poor Paddy. Poor sweet boy," she said aloud, carefully placing the article back in the book and then turning to Chapter One.

Five and a half hours later, having downed an additional four cups of tea and the remains of the Danish, Natasha closed the book with a sense of immense satisfaction. Her identification with Alexandra Bergson, the main character, was complete. Natasha had raced through the final pages in fear for the heroine, but the novel did not disappoint.

She recalled Paddy telling her, 'It's about immigrants and I really loved it.' Right then she knew she'd love it, too. And despite the tennis silliness, there was something about Patrick Donnelly that struck her as truthful and sincere.

But what about the doggie bag? He obviously had taken it. There was simply no other plausible explanation. But did she care? Was she offended? *Hardly*, she thought, picking at the crumbs of her employer's former pastry. She and Paddy were partners in petty larceny. Very petty, it seemed to her.

Natasha spent the next hour reviewing Paddy's writing pads. *I need a plan*, she thought. She opened her computer and Googled *'New York City White Pages.'*

"It's for sure you can't go back to the deli," Jimmy said.

"Right. That's out. Burned my bridges."

"So, how do you find her? Natasha, is it?"

"Yes, Natasha. But no last name."

"Did she tell you anything about herself?"

"I only know that she likes tennis."

"Well then. Maybe you could try and find her at the tennis court?"

"Are you daft, Jim? I already checked on-line. Only about nine thousand places in New York where you can play tennis."

"Right then. How about stopping by the deli at the close of her shift? Try to catch her. Apologize for the doggie bag. Might that work?"

Paddy finished folding the last linen napkin into a swan. "Unless I can think of something better."

Only two of the six Patrick Donnellys listed in the White Pages were at home. One too young. One too old. And she could tell from the recorded messages that the remaining four were obviously not *her* Patrick Donnelly. No baritones. No brogues.

But rather than disappointment, Natasha felt relieved. *Won't have to talk to him quite yet. Give me more time to figure out an approach. And if I reach him, what then? What do I say? If I tell him I've got his writing tablets, he'll know for sure I've read them. I could just skip over that and tell him I finished O Pioneers and that I really loved it. Ask him if he wants the book back. He might say, 'How 'bout coming by, dropping it off?' 'Sure, I say.' I go on over. I knock. He answers the door. 'Here's your book,' I say. Then what do I do? Do I tell him, 'I really like you? Can we go to bed right now and get the sex out of the way? Then we can talk, get to know each other.' No. No. No. What are you thinking, girl? He'd lose his smitten-ness. If I come on to him too quickly he might be disappointed. That's the last thing I want to do.*

There remained one more possibility in the White Pages, a P. Donnelly. Natasha dialed.

"I'll go to the deli tomorrow, late afternoon. I think her shift is over at five. I can hang around on the street. Then when she comes out, I'll go up to her. I'll apologize for the doggie bag. I'll confess. She'll forgive me. Then I'll tell her straight away that . . . that . . . "

"That what?" asked Jimmy.

Paddy sat up straight. "The truth. That I'm mad for her. That I think she's the grandest woman in the world. That I'd go to the ends of the earth for her." Paddy looked across the bar. "Think that'll work, Jim?"

"Well, it's rather bold. Could set her off some. Were it me, I believe I'd tone it down a mite. Soft pedal a bit."

Paddy slumped down again. "Right you are, Jim. If I come on too strong, she'll think I'm a typical New York lothario."

Jimmy raised his eyebrows. "Lothario, is it? No Paddy, dear. Needn't worry about that. No way you could be mistaken for one of them."

"Yeah?" The voice—female, young, Irish.

"Hello, I'm looking for Paddy Donnelly. Is he there?"

"Who wants him? Who are you? Is this Maureen?" the woman asked suspiciously.

"No. No. I'm not Maureen. My name's Natasha. I met Paddy yesterday and I have something to return to him. A book he loaned me."

A longish pause. "Alright. I'm his sister, Portia. If you want to drop it off at my place, he stops by regularly. I live in Brighton Beach."

"Thanks, that's kind of you, but I'd rather deliver it to him directly. And Brighton Beach is far from here. I'm in the Bronx, in Riverdale."

"Well that makes it even easier. Riverdale's not that far from where he works, in Brooklyn. *Tibor's Old Budapest,* a Hungarian restaurant just a couple blocks from Prospect Park. He's there tonight. *Tibor's*. You can Google Map it. T I B O R S. Got it?"

"Yes. I've got it. Thanks so very much," Natasha said. "Is he a cook?"

"No way. He's just a waiter. Almost a singing waiter. Good luck." Portia signed off.

Natasha rose and began pacing around the small kitchen. *Pioneers, dreamers,* she thought. And with that, her breathing slowed and her shoulders relaxed. She stood a little straighter.

"Did she show up yet?" Portia asked anxiously into the phone.

"Did who show up yet?" Paddy answered.

"The woman. What's her name?"

"What woman, Porsh? Who are you talking about?"

"The woman with your book. The one you loaned her. She's bringing it to you. To the restaurant. Tonight. I think her name's Natasha."

"Holy Mother of Mercy," Paddy whispered.

Natasha arrived at *Tibor's* just past eight. She had taken special care with her appearance—less waitressy, more feminine: dark slacks, a deep blue turtleneck sweater, a cream colored jacket, and her hair, unbraided, loose-flowing.

Her initial peek-through-the-doors survey into the restaurant revealed a packed old world eatery with heavy tables, dark wood paneling, large potted shrubs, paintings of the Danube on the walls, and a snug bar along one side. The *maître d'* let her know that there wasn't a table to be had and suggested she wait at the bar. Since she wanted to remain as inconspicuous as possible while she worked out her plan, an end seat at the bar was the perfect place. She'd be able to observe the entire restaurant from a position of relative concealment.

The bartender, alerted by this striking looking woman, and thinking she might be *the one*, appeared immediately.

"Hi. What'll it be?" Jimmy asked.

"Actually, I'm here to find someone."

Just as he was about to inquire whether that 'someone' might be his best friend, and if she might be called Natasha, the doors to the kitchen swung open and Paddy emerged, balancing a tray on his shoulder and carrying a small folding table in the other hand. He eased into the room, deftly dodged another waiter, and began wending his way expertly between tables.

Graceful. He's probably a good dancer, she thought, watching his progress through the restaurant. Paddy arrived at his destination, snapped open the folding table, placed the tray carefully down, then quickly distributed the entrees to a family of four—parents and kids. After passing out the dishes, he knelt down between the two children and proceeded to point out things on their plates, obviously explaining what they had ordered. Natasha was too far away to hear but she saw how charmed they all were by his efforts. Smiles and thanks were showered on him as he rose, and then started back to the kitchen. On his way, a well-dressed man came up to him and spoke briefly. Paddy nodded and changed direction, moving now toward the small bandstand at the rear of the restaurant.

"That'd be Tibor, the owner," Jimmy said to Natasha. "Probably suggesting that it's time for the evening's poetry recital. In Hungarian, if you can believe it." Jimmy looked closely at the woman seated across from him. "You'd be Natasha, am I right?"

"Yes. How'd you know?"

"Portia called. We've all been waiting for you."

Before she could respond, several of the diners, alerted by seeing Paddy approach the bandstand, began to chant, "Pad-dy, A-dy. Pad-dy, A-dy." They quieted down when he gained the riser.

"Thanks so much, friends," Paddy began. "As all you regulars here at Tibor's know, our favorite Hungarian poet is Endre Ady. With your kind permission I'd like to recite for you one of his poems. It's called *I Guard Your Eyes*. Please forgive me, in advance, for my poor pronunciation."

As Paddy gazed down onto the stage, gathering inspiration, his focus was interrupted when one of the diners, sitting close to the bandstand, tipped over his glass of beer, spilling half the contents on the floor.

"Not to worry," Paddy rushed to assure the disappointed and embarrassed diner. "Another is on the way, even as we speak." He signaled to Jimmy.

The bartender was already pouring the replacement, and at the same time began tilting his head in Natasha's direction. Paddy took his friend's hint, looked to the other end of the bar, saw *her*, took a step backward, and fell at once into a deep trance. Dumbfounded. Speechless. Immobilized.

The diners looked to see what had riveted the waiter's attention. They saw a lovely, russet-haired woman waving sweetly to the man on the bandstand and wearing a smile that seemed to ignite the entire room.

The diners looked back at Paddy. Then once again at Natasha, still beaming. After several seconds, one of the customers broke the silence, "Are you going to wave back, Paddy or stand there like a doofus?" Others began to encourage him. "Wave Paddy. Quick, before she leaves."

Goaded on by the helpful diners, the waiter finally

awakened, managed a small wave and found his voice. "Friends," he spoke quietly to the diners. "The young woman at the end of the bar is called Natasha." He hesitated, shaking his head. "I've been lost for a good while, but she's found me tonight. In her honor and for her sake, I'd like to take a short break from Endre Ady, our favorite Hungarian poet. Instead, I'd like to recite a short poem by William Butler Yeats, our favorite Irish poet. It's called, *To an Isle in the Water*.

Never taking his eyes off of Natasha, Paddy began:

> *Shy one, shy one,*
> *Shy one of my heart,*
> *She moves in the firelight*
> *Pensively apart.*
>
> *She carries in the dishes,*
> *And lays them in a row.*
> *To an isle in the water*
> *With her would I go.*
>
> *She carries in the candles,*
> *And lights the curtained room,*
> *Shy in the doorway*
> *And shy in the gloom;*
> *And shy as a rabbit,*
> *Helpful and shy.*
> *To an isle in the water*
> *With her would I fly.*

A mesmerizing silence. Then bursting, thunderous applause, stamping, whistling, shouts of 'hooray,' and 'bravo,' the diners alternately looking at Paddy and Natasha, whose smile, if possible, had grown even more radiant.

The waiter acknowledged the crowd with a nodded *'thanks,'* and with eyes still glued on the object of his enchantment, stepped off the platform and headed in her direction. He had taken barely two strides before his sneakers found the beer. What happened next would become one of the restaurant's enduring legends, recalled fondly by all of Tibor's regulars who were there to witness the event: a classic pratfall—Paddy's legs going out from under him. Arms flailing skyward. His body coming parallel to the floor. A momentary suspension of time. Then gravity taking over, crashing the waiter onto his backside, stunned.

The crowd gasped in unison and quickly rushed assistance.

After a minute, still groggy, Paddy opened his eyes and gazed up into the face of his favorite waitress. She was cradling his head in her lap, gently rubbing his temples.

Natasha looked down at him and smiled. "Doggie bag?" she asked.

Paddy looked up at her, grinning like a fool. "Not me," he said. "Must have been Sharapova."

As she burst out laughing, one of her auburn tresses fell forward, lightly sweeping across his face.

Heaven, Paddy thought.

#

A Conversation

THE YOUNGER OF the two men sniffed at his glass of rioja and smiled encouragingly across the small table. "So. How often, would you say?"

The other man, considerably older, thinning and graying on top, seemed uncomfortable with the question. He hesitated, wagging his head. Finally, after half a minute, "Dunno, mate. Not very often."

The younger man nodded. "OK. 'Often' is perhaps too relative a term. I mean, often for one person might be infrequently for another. Right?"

"I s'pose."

"So let me rephrase," the questioner said gently. "Do you have sex with your wife once a week? That's pretty definite."

The older man stared down at his hands, resting in his lap. He shrugged his shoulders then looked up, meeting the other's eyes. "No. Not that often."

The younger man allowed several seconds to elapse. "No? Ok. How 'bout once a month?"

"Even less frequently than that," the older man answered, more quickly this time.

The questioner picked up his wine glass, examined the last swallow, and tossed it down. He held up the empty and spoke loudly, projecting out across the small, riverside bodega. "Senor," he called to the waiter. "Por favor. Otra vez, por favor."

The waiter acknowledged the man with a nod and disappeared through swinging doors.

The questioner turned back to the older man with a 'where were we?' expression on his face.

The older man appeared more relaxed. "Well, I was just

telling you that I don't have sex with my wife on a monthly basis. But . . . I'm curious. Why this interest in my sex life? I mean, we met only a few minutes ago and here we are jumping right into the thick of things. A bit dodgy, don't you think?"

"Sorry. So sorry," the questioner said, leaning forward. "I should have told you right away. I'm a psychiatrist. A Freudian, actually. I have a practice outside of London. I'm here in Salamanca for a conference. Be here for a week. Conference begins on Tuesday and I'm to deliver the keynote."

The analyst sat back in his chair and surveyed the almost empty café before turning back to the other man. "I've pretty much mapped out what I want to talk about: the sex drive in older men. How they might see themselves differently from when they were younger. Whether they feel themselves as driven as they might have felt at one time. That sort of thing. It's a talk I've given many times. But to tell the truth, lately I find it a little . . . I don't know. Stale, I dare say. Definitely stale. So, I'm trying to freshen it up a bit, trying to find first-hand anecdotal commentary from individuals, older men, like yourself. Men with whom I've spoken face to face. Not simply men whose views have been collected and catalogued and are now somehow expressed, numerically or percentage-wise, in some kind of god-awful PowerPoint graph. But men who might provide their *personal* slant on things. Follow?"

The older man was listening carefully. "Right. Makes sense. But how did you know I'd be willing to talk to you?"

"Pretty obvious right away whether someone will be responsive."

"How's that?"

"Well, most men, when asked by a complete stranger

—someone they've just met in a café or in a pub, as you and I have just met—about the details of their sexual relations with their wives, they usually respond pretty predictably: 'That's really none of your business, old chap.' Or, 'I'd rather not discuss the personal side of my sex life, if you don't mind.' Or, 'Sod off, mate.' Something like that. But once in a while —tonight as an example, here with you—I bump into someone who doesn't mind talking. They might not be eager, but at least they don't mind sharing. Especially after I've identified myself as a Freudian." The analyst smiled, shaking his head. "People generally tend to believe that Freud is all about sex. It seems to make it easier for some men to open up."

As the waiter delivered the therapist's new glass of wine, the older man's cell phone went off. He picked it up, recognized the number, then quickly pressed the green button and spoke. "Hello love." A long pause and a glowing smile while the man listened intently. "Yes, darling. Definitely. No. Not to worry. I'll be there. Promise. Absolutely." Now grinning broadly and in an almost whispery tone: "I'm looking forward to it, too. See you soon. 'Bye." He closed his cell phone and looked at the analyst. "Sophie," he announced in a tone that seemed to the speaker to need no further explanation.

"Sophie?" the Freudian said. "Your wife?"

The older man recoiled. "Oh no. No. No. No. Sophie is . . . she isn't . . . Sophie is *not* my wife," he sputtered, exhaling loudly and letting his gaze drift outside the window next to their table. Several rowboats—an improvised regatta—were floating languidly on the Rio Tormes, down the embankment from the bodega. Young men were rowing young women. All were dressed warmly, the winter sun providing little heat. From one of the boats, light guitar music floated across the water.

Now the older man turned again to the psychiatrist and straightened in his chair. "Sophie, actually, is . . . she's . . . well. She's *my lover*." The speaker's eyebrows shot up and he sat back, the pronouncement surprising even he, himself. "I'm not sure I've ever said that to anyone. Must be because you're a Freudian," he laughed.

"See. I told you," the analyst said," returning the man's smile. "We're easy to talk to. We're all about sex." The psychiatrist lifted his wine glass and toasted the speaker. "Thanks for being so honest with me."

The other man tipped his glass toward the psychiatrist, returning the toast. "I guess the cat's out of the bag now. So . . . in for a penny and all that." The man took a swallow of wine, breathed in deeply, and began. "We've had a long run, Sophie and me. Going on thirteen, fourteen years now. We try and break away and see each other as often as possible. Best we can do is a couple times a year. If we're lucky." He looked out the window again. "Actually, we met right across the river, on the promenade, in 2004. You can see the spot from here. That small grove of cork trees. See?" He pointed toward a wooded promontory that jutted into the river.

"Yes, I see the spot. Lovely," the analyst said.

Seemingly emboldened by his description of his extra-marital lover, the older man now hastened to fill in the details. "Sophie's also married. Long time. To Douglas. Bit of a wanker, but not a bad sort, really. Works for Barclays in Sheffield. We all met when we were here in Spain, on holiday. One of those five-day Thomas Cook packages out of Heathrow. She with Doug. Me with Jen. Jen's the wife."

The Freudian reached into his briefcase and withdrew a small pad and pen. He looked questioningly across the table.

"Mind if I take notes?"

"I guess not. You going to use this in your talk?"

"Yes, I'd like to, especially since you seem so forthcoming about the intimate side of your life. But only with your permission."

The other man took hold of his glass and slid it back and forth, slowly and carefully, over the starched-smooth tablecloth. "No. No, I guess I don't mind. You won't use my real name, though, will you?"

"Certainly not. No one will ever know your real name. We don't normally even *use* names when describing our conversations."

Just at that moment, two forty-ish women, one dressed in red, the other in lavender, reeled into the bodega. They each carried a glass of wine and were laughing hysterically. The one in lavender mis-stepped and sloshed her drink all down the side of the other's red dress. They both howled with delight. The waiter came over and steered them to a small table at the far side of the bodega. Almost immediately upon taking their seats, their laughter died down and they lapsed into a serious silence.

The psychiatrist's attention focused back on the older man. He opened his pad and took up his pen. "You were saying you don't have sex with your wife . . . Jennifer, right? . . . even once a month. Have I got it?"

"Pretty much. Though at the beginning we went at it like rabbits—three, four times a week. But that tapered off rather quickly. And not long into our marriage, we'd sometimes go months at a time without sex."

"Did your tapering off coincide with you meeting Sophie?"

"No. Not at all. It was mostly because neither Jen nor I enjoyed having sex with the other. Pretty simple, really." The older man closed his eyes and collected himself. In a quiet voice, "I was much younger then and didn't know as much as I do now about women's needs and all. But I'm better now," he said slowly, positively, opening his eyes. "All thanks to Sophie. She's been super patient with me. We enjoy each other tremendously."

The psychiatrist took notes, sipping his wine. "And what about Jennifer? You said she excited you in the beginning."

"Sure. At first. But I realized, a year into the marriage —that would have been almost twenty-five years ago—that she'd rather sleep than have sex." The older man hesitated before continuing. "Sex didn't seem important to her. At least sex with *me*. It's entirely possible—probable, really—that she'd love sex with another bloke. And you know what? I'd *love* for her to find someone. Really, I would. Jen's a good person. She deserves to have a sexual relationship as satisfying as the one I'm having with Sophie."

The analyst looked up from his pad. "That's generous of you. Normally men tend to be very narrow, very possessive. Have you suggested such an arrangement to her? An open marriage?"

Shouts burst from across the room. One of the women began demanding something of the other. The men's attention was drawn to them.

"What's the problem over there?" the Freudian asked. "Do you speak Spanish well enough to understand?"

The older man lifted a hand, shushing the psychiatrist, at the same time inclining slightly toward the women. After a minute, "They seem to be lovers. The one who was shouting, the one in red, accused the other of being unfaithful. With a man, not with another woman. The one in violet denied it. She said that after all they had been through together, the shouter had a lot of nerve accusing *her* of infidelity, especially after what happened last year."

"What happened last year?" whispered the Freudian.

"Don't know. They only referred to some incident in Barcelona, in January."

As suddenly as they had erupted, the two women calmed down. The one who was shouted at reached across the table and took the hand of the other woman. They were silent for a moment. The shouter removed her hand from the grasp of the other, took up her glass of wine and finished it off. She gathered her handbag and shawl and stood up. The other woman also rose. Silently, they walked out of the bodega, holding hands.

"Whatever was going on," the Freudian said, "looks like they sorted things out."

"Sometimes you can do that. Sometimes you can't." His cell phone rang again. He looked to see who was calling. "Damn," he frowned. "It's Jen. I'm tempted not to answer."

"Jennifer? You mean she's *here* in Salamanca, along with Sophie?"

"Yes, unfortunately. Makes for a lot of sneaking around. No fun for Sophie. She's here alone. Doug's back home in Sheffield doing his ledgers."

The two men stared at the phone. It rang four more times then stopped. There was no voice mail message.

"Complicated," the analyst said. He looked down at his note pad. "We were talking about the possibility of having an open marriage. You and Jennifer. Did that ever come up?"

The older man looked at his watch. "Listen. I've got to go. Sophie can only spare a couple of hours and Jen thinks I've gone to Valladolid on business for the day. It's hell conniving like this." The older man hesitated. "No. No. We haven't really spoken about an open marriage. I don't think it would work out."

"Why's that? Wouldn't it be more honest and make it easier for you and Sophie?"

"Not really. See, Doug, Sophie's husband, isn't well. He's really a bundle of nerves. He'd probably lie down and die if she were to tell him about us. No, it's probably better this way. The truth would be far more painful for the two spouses. Sophie and I have talked about it a lot. We both agree that this is the best way. For now." He stood, took a final sip from his wine and began to reach for his wallet.

"No, please," said the analyst, "allow me. It's the least I can do. You've been so generous with your time."

The older man inclined his head and offered his hand across the table. "It's been a good thing to be able to share with you. I feel somehow . . . relieved, I guess is the word."

"Goodbye, then," said the Freudian, taking the other man's hand. "And good luck to you and to Sophie. And to Jennifer."

The older man nodded a 'thanks' then turned and walked out of the bodega just as a large crowd of tourists surged in. They began shouting for immediate service. The tables surrounding the analyst quickly filled. When the scene had quieted down, the psychiatrist took out his cell phone, dialed, and spoke briefly. Twenty minutes later, an attractive, middle-aged woman entered, stopped at the doorway and began searching. She didn't see the analyst right away. But he saw her and stood up and waved and called out to her, shouting over the din, "Jennifer darling, I'm here."

The woman saw him and rushed to his table, smiling radiantly. "At last, my dearest," she said, falling into his waiting arms. "I've had a devil of time getting away."

#

Holy Writ

THE FIRST TIME the stranger showed up at services—that would have been about five weeks earlier by Pastor Wyndham's reckoning—he had failed to take notes. Didn't even pick up a pencil. An oversight most of the faithful either ignored or ascribed to an unfamiliarity with *Order 6* of Holy Writ.

That first time—a Thursday night's *Blessing of the Word* —had otherwise been largely uneventful, notwithstanding Abner Grayson's constant, almost out-loud, bleating of the *Ten Essential Fonts.*

Pastor Wyndham had been away most of the day searching—vainly as it turned out—for printed matter. He returned only late in the afternoon, barely an hour before *Convocation.*

"Hardly had time to blow his nose," said Writey Wayne, the Pastor's ancient housekeeper, explaining why that evening's services were over so quickly. "He was writin' *The Five Sacred Placards* while he was still puttin' on his cassock," she said afterwards.

Ira Banks, never a partisan of Pastor Wyndham, wasn't satisfied. "How come he used the *littler* placards?" the carpenter asked no one in particular. "And why he done gone and used Bodoni, tonight of all nights, only Gutenberg, (*"Blessed Be The Name"*) might be able to tell us," Banks added testily.

The next time the stranger came to services—on the third Sunday in March—he sat closer to the high altar.

"Close enough to be able to read *The Blessed Phrase* on Pastor Wyndham's lectern *and* to copy it down. Which'en he did *not* do," John Farlight told several of his friends afterwards. "She'it, if I coulda reddit with my own eyes and copied it on Sacred Yellow Pad—and I was settin' two rows *behind* the stranger—no way *he* couldn'ta."

Farlight's friends sagely nodded in agreement. None of them, however, was willing to admit that, had they been in the stranger's row, or in *any* row for that matter, not one of them would have been able to read *or* copy down the message written on the Pastor's lectern. And not for lack of visual acuity, but rather because of iSFEARS.[1]

During the next Sunday's *Gloria Punctuatum*, (*"If we forget our commas and colons, O Lord, dele our names from your Sacred Tablets)* the stranger's continuing failure to copy down Holy Writ drew a few stares, mostly from Ira Banks and his kin. Not that dirty looks from the Banks brood was anything to fret about.

"Brown nosin', no-'count, an-alphabet-niks," John Farlight had long ago dubbed the Banks clan. "They be settin' close to the Pastor for years now, hopin' some lit'racy'll rub off. But that dog won' hunt," Farlight laughed derisively.

As the congregants filed out after the *Gloria*, the stranger was the subject of a handful of post-*Convocation* musings.

"Why was the newcomer a-holdin' back?" Sarah Mayhew asked her sister, Angie. "I mean, there was pencil and Sacred Yellow Pad in front o' him. I know. I put in a sharpen'd half dozen Number 2 Papermates (*"Blessed Be The Name")* in that very row, the one he was a-settin' in."

Angie, the more devout of the pair, did not speak. The

---

[1] iPod Small Font Eye Alienation/Reduction Syndrome. A visual disorder brought on by continually staring at 5 point type on teensy screens. The reader gradually loses the ability to distinguish individual letters, *of any size*. The disorder is congenital and becomes incurable in the third generation.

woman took her vows more seriously than Sarah, and would guard her silence for the prescribed three hours from the time Pastor Wyndham ended *Convocation* and intoned *The Parting*, (*"Go now, be silent, and think on the word"*). In just a few hours, Angie would speak her mind. But now, on their way home through ankle-deep snow, she kept her thoughts to herself.

At the following Saturday morning's *Readings for the Ready*, the stranger showed up early and sat himself down in the middle of a still empty second row. Then, according to Deacon Don Crowley—who had arrived early to pass out erasers— "The stranger done closed his eyes and looked up into the ceilin', smilin' as if Holy Writ were flowin' plumb through his eyeballs. I never seed nothin' like it. Just settin' there with his eyes shet. Big as Faro readin' his hy-ro-glifficks," Crowley concluded, not having the faintest notion what or who Faro was. Forget about the hy-ro-glifficks.

A few minutes later, the morning's group of *Ready Readers* began to file in and take their seats. Most gave the stranger a wide berth, so that when the tall man finally opened his eyes and looked about him, he saw an almost empty row. The only *Ready Reader* sitting close by was Elder Josiah Breeden, close to ninety and one of the last survivors of the Fourth Web War, the one that finally (*"Thanks Be To The Holy Deity")* put an end to electronic information.

Josiah had participated in the twenty-six day siege of the New York Public Library's Mid-Manhattan branch, the last to fall to the An-Alphabet-Niks (AAN). As a founding member of the urban guerrilla group, *Bold Print*, Elder Breeden had defended the library until it was clear the AAN was gaining the upper hand. Before that fateful, now celebrated day—

December 3, 2049—Breeden, and what remained of the *Bold Print* fighters, managed to smuggle out of the branch library a small handful of books, including the entire *Hardy Boys* series, *The Naked Lunch, Yertle the Turtle, The DaVinci Code, The Seven Habits of Highly Effective People,* and *The Art of the Deal,* all of which now formed the required reading core of their church's *Most Sacred Texts.*

Elder Breeden rarely missed a *Convocation*, celebrating even the lesser holidays: MLA Day, Strunk and White Week, and even the Feast of Kanji (They were, after all, a non-denominational church). And although they couldn't make head nor tail of that Asia scribbling—wherever the hell Asia was supposed to be—they gave the alphabet its due. "Even if a bunch of damn fur'ners done gone and writ it. Amen," said Todd Banks, Ira's dim-witted eldest son.

Josiah leaned toward the stranger and nodded a 'hello.' The man smiled back and inclined his bald head in a return greeting, his dark green eyes joyful. Elder Breeden moved closer to the stranger, taking a seat next to the man.

During Pastor Wyndham's sermon—a homily on sans serif fonts—the stranger took a Sacred Yellow Pad and a Papermate No. 2, and began writing. Josiah read along, nodding and chuckling in agreement.

"What'd he write?" Rebecca Farlight demanded. She and half the town had gathered in the foyer of their church after services.

"No one knows," said Deacon Don Crowley. "He dint deposit his writin' after *Convocation*."

"What? He dint…?" shouted half a dozen incredulous voices.

"Who the hell he think he be?" Luellen Banks, one of Ira's three wives, demanded.

"That's anti-Writ, if I ever know'd of sech of thing," Sarah Mayhew offered.

"Calm down, everyone," Pastor Wyndham's voice cut through the hubbub. "Calm down and let's figgur' out what's goin' on here."

The Pastor strode into the roiling midst of his parishioners. He was still wearing his cassock and purple beanie. And he was holding aloft his oaken *Alpha Chain*, the beaded necklace of twenty–nine small wooden cubes with a letter of the English alphabet carved into the sides of twenty-six of the cubes.[2]

The parishioners fell back in the presence of the raised talisman. They lowered their heads, dropped their eyes, and ceded center stage to their spiritual leader.

Wyndham surveyed his flock with a look that was, at the same time, haughty and indulgent. "My children," he began. "Let's not pre-jedge this here stranger. Let's jes' gather together and try to figgur' out who he be, why he's a-come, and what danger, if any, he might pose to our congregation. First off, we need to know more 'bout him."

"Right" said the obsequious Ira Banks. "The Pastor's right. We need to know who the 'F' this stranger be."

Who the F?, where the F?, and what the F? were some of Ira's favorite expressions. He had heard the phrases

---

[2] A confusion about the number of letters in the English alphabet arose about the time of The Conflagration, the two decades that followed the fall of the Mid-Manhattan Library in which the AAN systemically attempted to destroy all printed matter found in America. The Synod of Orthographers, established in 2087, issued a preliminary bull in which three new letters (ñ, ö, and ç) are being considered for inclusion into the English alphabet. Hence, the addition of the three blank cubes on all Alpha Chains

years earlier and continued to use them, believing they gave a *'literate'* color to his limited verbal abilities. When pressed to explain their meaning, Ira always assumed an aggrieved posture. "Why'd you be wantin' to know?" he'd ask belligerently.

The Pastor caught John Farlight's eye for the briefest second. They silently expressed to each other their shared distaste for Banks.

"Thank you Ira," the Pastor said smoothly. "And may Saints Cyril and Methodius be a blessin' 'pon you," he intoned gravely.

The rest of the faithful, eyes still lowered, echoed, *"Amen."*

The Pastor repeated his question. "Who be this here stranger? Where he be a-stayin'?"

The congregants looked blankly at each other, waiting for someone to step forward. Finally, from the rear of the crowd, Emmie Ann Breeden, Josiah's youngest granddaughter, spoke out. "We be takin' care of him. Granddad and me," she said. "Been stayin' in our barn. He and Granddad talk a lot. Nice feller."

The stranger was just finishing up with his journal's latest entry, a set of four short poems he planned to share with the townspeople at the following Monday's *Writing is for Everyone.* He paused when he heard the crunch of snow-trod on the narrow wooden bridge connecting his host's property with the edge of town. He could make out a low rumble of voices, voices that did not seem to him to be as full of joy as he would have liked. The stranger closed the small notebook and placed it in his shirt pocket. He put on a heavy overcoat and a broad-brimmed, dark gray hat, took up his kerosene lamp, and went out from the barn. He walked through a gentle snowfall toward the approaching crowd, several of whom carried sputtering torches.

The stranger paused at the corral gate to hang his lamp, its light dimly illuminating the newly carpeted snow-white yard in front of the barn. In the corral, two dun colored horses softly nickered. One came close to nuzzle the man. The stranger gently stroked the dun's neck, brushing off the few snowflakes that had collected on the horse's mane.

As they came closer, the crowd's massed mutterings lost some of their fervor. They quieted down and stopped about ten feet from the tall man. Emmie Ann Breeden came out of the crowd and walked forward. "Evenin' Mister," she said, formally but kindly. "Granddad home?"

The stranger bowed gentlemanly to Emmie Ann and indicated with a nod of his head that Josiah was in the main house. She grinned sunnily up at the man and turned toward her home. The stranger surveyed the crowd and nodded to them, smiling a greeting, then waited for a reply. A minute passed. Then another. When no response was forthcoming, the man reached into his pocket and took out his small notebook, opened it and riffed through the pages until he found what he wanted. The crowd was mesmerized by his actions. He looked at them, inclined his notebook toward the wan light of the kerosene lamp, closed his eyes as if receiving Holy Writ and began to speak:

"In a darkling time,
Came I to read thee a verse.
But no one harkened."

The few voices that had persisted in the crowd now fell silent, struck as much by the stranger's words as by the richness of his deep voice, a voice that all were now hearing for the first time. They stared at the man, not knowing what to make of the haunting and mysterious words, spoken so solemnly and yet "with sech a feelin' o' love," Angie Mayhew would later recount to her sister.

Standing at the head of the crowd, Pastor Wyndham felt himself at a loss. Finally, he was able to take a step forward and asked the man, not without a tinge of threat in his tone, "What is yer meanin', stranger? Who you be and why have you come?"

Even by the pale and flickering light of the lamp and the half dozen crackling torches held aloft by some in the crowd, the man's green eyes seemed to grow more lustrous. They looked directly at Wyndham and held the holy man's gaze. When the pastor finally looked away, the stranger again took up his notebook:

> *"Bowing down your heads*
> *To uncaring, false prophets*
> *Is the way of slaves."*

Pastor Wyndham looked up with a startled expression and took a step back. The air around him now seemed charged. The crowd sensed it, as if smelling the ozone before the lightning. And for all they knew, a bolt might very well strike their religious leader. They drew back from him lest they, too, be consumed. The pastor searched their faces, seeking some support. All eyes now dared to look into his. Wyndham turned back to the stranger and demanded, in a voice filled with venom and fear, "Who you think you be?"

The stranger took a step toward Wyndham and gently reached out a hand to the frightened man. But the pastor drew back.

"I am who I am," the tall man pronounced.

Wyndham recoiled. He had heard that phrase somewhere in the past but could not remember where. He continued to back away from the tall man, as if being repulsed by a force that seemed to surround the stranger. The crowd parted and let their pastor withdraw. He turned and disappeared into a sudden snow flurry. His steps could be heard hurriedly retreating. The crowd now refocused its attention on the stranger and drew closer to him.

"Speak agin, sir," said John Farlight quietly.

The stranger walked to Farlight, placed a hand on his shoulder and spoke to him directly. "Heed me, John:

> *"Much better it is*
> *To howl at the angry wind*
> *Than pray to mute fonts."*

Then the man turned to the crowd and raised his arms skyward and thundered in his rolling voice:

> *"I ask: when again*
> *Will the word be beautiful?*
> *Will you allow it?"*

Sensing the majesty of the moment, the townspeople fell to their knees and clasped their hands in front of them. The men removed their hats. Everyone looked up into the man's dark green eyes and waited in reverential silence for further enlightenment. A moment later, Emmie Ann Breeden, as if on cue, came out of the house carrying a wide wicker basket. She made her way through the crowd, walked up to the tall man and knelt down.

"Granddad said this here's fer you, stranger. He done offered five silver coins and two gold'ns. And here's my mama's ring." She placed the basket on the snow in front of the man. He reached down and placed his hand on her head. She let it rest there a moment, then took his palm to her lips. The stranger helped Emmie to her feet. She went quickly back to the house.

John Farlight watched her go and then turned to the crowd with wide eyes. He rose up and came forward. Reaching into his pants pocket, he pulled out a handful of coins, dropped them into the basket, and received the stranger's blessed palm on his head.

One by one the crowd followed Farlight's example.

When it was Angie Mayhew's turn, she quietly admitted, "Ain't got no money, mister. But I got these," she said, taking off two jeweled charm bracelets and dropping them into the stranger's palm.

Several women added necklaces. Some men gave silver *Alpha Chains*. Ira Banks approached the man and laid an ancient gold, filigreed pocket watch in the basket.

The stranger smiled warmly at Ira. "You will be with me always," he spoke. Ira grinned hugely and looked around to his fellow townspeople. "You heerd 'im. I'll be with 'im always." Ira floated back into the crowd.

When all had added their contributions and all had been blessed, the tall man spoke again.

"Go now home and sleep.
Tomorrow prepare a feast.
We will all partake."

The crowd slowly dispersed, glancing back as they drew away. The stranger remained standing where they had left him, limned in white by the falling snow, his arms stretched out to them.

The next day dawned blue and golden. It had snowed throughout the night but by daybreak, the last flake had fallen and the sky lightened into the purest, cloudless cerulean. A freshening, warm wind seemed to breathe spring onto the countryside. A single crocus, sitting alone under a sheltering eave, burst open—a deep purple flash.

By noontime, people began gathering in the church, bringing the food they had prepared for the promised feast. Pastor Wyndham's absence went mostly unremarked. When all had gathered, they began to walk the mile to Josiah Breeden's home.

Carrying pies and cakes, stews and soups, fresh breads and biscuits, they began a barely remembered melody. "It's a hymn, a church song," Sarah Mayhew said. "Amazin' . . . sumpin'," she said. No one knew the words but the beautiful tune she hummed was easily learned.

They arrived a half hour later at the Breeden farm. John Farlight went up to the door, knocked and called out, "Josiah. Emmie. Stranger. We've come to feast." The ensuing silence was broken only by the occasional crunch of snow as someone stepped around his neighbor to see better. Soon, people began to shift nervously.

"Lookie there," said Ira Banks, pointing to the barn door where a piece of paper fluttered ever so slightly in the breeze.

John Farlight put down his pot of rabbit stew and walked slowly toward the barn, passing a now empty corral. Without taking the note off of the nail that held it to the door, Farlight read to himself.

"What's it say, John? Read the note," several in the crowd demanded, coming closer. Farlight took the paper off the door and looked at his neighbors, now gathered in a semi-circle around him.

"It's a short note. Says, 'There's one born every minute.' I don't get it. One what?"

Ira Banks turned a mystified face to Sarah Mayhew. "What the 'F' does it mean, Sarah?"

#

Outta the Blue

RUFUS TILLEY WAS enjoying lunch at the Loma Alta Cafe on Main Street, catty-corner from Carl's Food Hop. He was half way through the diner's Wednesday Special— spaghetti and meatballs, garlic bread, vinaigrette salad, and iced tea—when Gwen Erickson burst through the eatery's door and began flailing demonstratively, the way she always did when she was excited. She searched a moment, spotted Tilley, then shouted across the restaurant, over the heads of the other diners, "Sheriff Tilley. Sheriff Tilley. Come quick. You're needed out at Morgan Winkler's farm. Pronto!"

All the luncheoners looked up from concentrating on their Wednesday Specials, some with strands of pasta, still un-souped up, dangling from their marinara-reddened lips. Their gazes tennis-courted from Gwen to Rufus, wondering what had happened at Winkler's.

The chief law enforcement officer of the corn-belt town of Carrier, Nebraska, stared at Gwen, standing there, flapping her arms up and down, her curly, straw blond hair spraying out in all directions from under her deputy's cap.

Never one to abandon a meal half-eaten, Tilley beckoned Gwen closer, showing her a seat opposite.

"Now then, Deputy Gwen, what exactly happened over at Morgan Winkler's that might be so goldarn important that I'd get up from this here delicious spaghetti lunch?"

"A man done fell through the Winkler's roof," she blurted.

Tilley regarded the young woman for a moment, then repeated in a jestful voice, "A man fell through the Winkler's roof?"

"That's right sheriff. Left a hole the size of a small John Deere in the cedar shakes, passed right on through BettyRae's sewing room on the second floor, and pretty much exploded in their kitchen on the first floor."

Tilley continued to stare, as did every customer within hearing distance. Several quickly got up, left money on their tables, and made for the exit, presumably to go and see for themselves the destruction caused by the falling man.

"Uh huh," Tilley said, using the last crust of garlic bread to sop up the remains of the marinara. "Might it have been a large hailstone? We've had some pretty unusual weather in these parts since Trump's been president."

"No sirree," Gwen said emphatically. "It were a man."

"And we know this because . . .?"

"Parts everywhere, sheriff. Human parts. Legs, arms. BettyRae said the man's head wound up in her kitchen sink, half buried in a bunch of fresh corn she was a fixin' to shuck. Said his eyes were open, a starin' right at her."

Two women diners sitting in a booth across from the sheriff covered their mouths with their hands, the Wednesday Special apparently on its way back up. One of them, Aggie Shelton, wife of Carl (Food Hop Carl) dashed for the rest room. Almost made it, too.

At the news of the body parts, Sheriff Tilley seemed convinced. He finished his iced tea, wiped his mouth, slid out of the booth and rose up, wheezing at the effort.

At a robust 270 pounds, Rufus Tilley was limited to slug-like locomotion, his speed influenced by cranky knees and by thirty-inch thighs that scraped chaffingly together when he walked. The sheriff belched long and loud, something he always did after lunch at the Loma. "Well, I guess we best get on over to Morgan Winkler's. See what the hell all the fuss is about."

A caressing zephyr skimmed over the prairie, making the corn sway and ripple as far as the eye could see. Atop Morgan Winkler's bright red barn a wind vane rooster squeaked its opposition to being continually re-directed this way and that.

By now, many of the townsfolk were on site, gawking, tsk-tsking, speculating on where the man had dropped from. The crowd's thinking had quickly gone in two directions: half the folks insisted the body must have fallen from a high-flying jet, else how could he have made such a prodigious hole in the Winkler roof. The other half was equally convinced that the victim had been ejected from an alien spacecraft after interstellar zombies had sucked the life force out of their captive earthling.

An ambulance from the Carrier Fire Department was parked nearby, Chief Jim Henry LaBoosh officiating. J.H. was directing two reluctant paramedics into putting on HAZMAT outfits, just in case the deceased might have become radioactive in his descent.

Sheriff Tilley and Deputy Erickson made a wide circuit around Winkler's home and surveyed the damage. The hole was as Gwen had described it—big enough to drive a small tractor clean through.

"From the puncture angle, I'm thinking the body fell from the north," Tilley suggested, pointing.

"But Sheriff Tilley," Gwen said. "I can't rightly 'member ever seeing *any* jets in the skies to the north o' Carrier."

Tilley looked down at the five foot, one inch, ninety-five pound Gwen. He rubbed his stomach. "Now that I think of it, Deputy Gwen, neither can I."

Being one of the first times her boss had ever found favor with anything she'd said, Gwen pushed on. "Maybe it weren't a *jet* plane the man fell outta. Maybe it were a small one, one of them mari-wanna delivery planes that fly between Herschel and St. Mark's."

Tilley appraised his young deputy. "I'll take that into consideration," he said. Gwen glowed.

"Meanwhile," the sheriff continued, "let's go check out those body parts."

Sheriff and deputy walked up onto the wraparound porch of the Winkler home.

A blubbering BettyRae was sitting on a large padded swing, a well-used white handkerchief balled in her lap. She was being comforted by Beau, her slow-thinking son.

"There, there, Momma," the boy drooled. "Ever'thang gonna be jes' fine 'n dandy."

Tilley and Gwen gave each other a knowing look and started for the front door. Their progress was arrested by the arrival of a shiny black SUV that screeched to a dusty halt in front of the Winkler home. The vehicle's four doors were flung open simultaneously and four men poured out, each a clone of the other: dark suits, dark ties, dark sunglasses, black shoes, buzz cut hair, not a smile between them.

"Lord Jesus," Tilley sighed. "It's the FBI." He looked down at Gwen and shook his head in dismay.

Each of the four men dropped into battle-ready squats, facing in different directions, as if gauging where an attack might come from. Then they looked to the sky, again in unison, searching the heavens for the next falling body. Satisfied that they were safe from an earthly or aerial blitz, they straightened and marched toward the house. One of them, clearly the leader of the pack, led the way. He was a short man, no more than five-foot four and thin as a rail. His chin jutted pugnaciously forward, eyes slitted, lips pursed. His pug nose twitched up and down, as if searching for a hint of cordite, but finding only the earthy aroma of cow pucky. He ignored the teary-eyed woman and slobbering young man and addressed the two local law enforcers. "I'm Agent Smith," the small man announced, offering the sheriff his badge.

Tilley had never seen an FBI badge. For all he knew, it could have come out of a box of Cracker Jacks. Nevertheless, the sheriff did his due diligence and inspected the proffered ID. "Appears to be authentic," he bluffed.

Agent Smith had stopped looking at Tilley and was gazing, transfixedly, at Gwen. *God, she's just my size,* the elfin agent thought.

For her part, Gwen was doing her best to look official. She stood tall next to her boss, one hand on her hip, the other resting comfortably on the butt of her holstered, S&W .357 Magnum Police Special, a gift from her daddy when she finished the academy in the state capital.

Agent Smith couldn't take his eyes off of the pixie blond. The three federal agents standing behind him began to fidget.

Then when Gwen squared her shoulders and her perky little nipples made an outdentation in her blouse, Agent Smith audibly gasped.

Sheriff Tilley had caught the interplay and sought to keep the rutting season at bay. He looked down at the federal squirt. "What might be the reason for your visit?"

Quantico took over and Smith snapped to. "We're here to investigate the report of a body falling outta the sky," he said.

Tilley could now discern a certain southern drawl in the federal runt's voice.

"That's what we're here for, too," the rotund sheriff said. "Let's go on in and check it out."

"We'll all go in," Smith said. "But the Bureau'll take jurisdiction."

"Hrummf," said Tilley.

"Bullshee-it," said Gwen.

Agent Smith thought he might be in love.

They were met at the door by Morgan Winkler. He was dressed in overalls, straw hat, and rubber boots that he hadn't properly wiped clean before entering his home, obvious because of the dung tracks on BettyRae's living room carpet.

"Rufus," Winkler sobbed. "Rufus, thank God you've come."

"Get 'hold of yourself, Morgan," Tilley advised. "And show us what in tarnation happened."

"Follow me."

As they piled through the living room and advanced toward the kitchen, Agent Smith managed to place himself next to Deputy Gwen. He held the kitchen's swinging door open for her. She smiled a 'thank you kindly' and nodded sweetly. She might even have winked.

He caught her scent: lilac and onion rings. His knees turned to jelly and he swooned. One of his minions grabbed him under the arms and righted the starry-eyed federal agent.

The kitchen was as Morgan Winkler had described, only worse, much worse. Yes, the farmer had properly noted the body parts—arms and legs, and such. And yes, he had described the man's head coming to rest in his wife's still unshucked corn, eyes staring blankly into space. But what Winkler had failed to mention was the hellacious amount of blood that coated every square inch of BettyRae's kitchen: walls, floor, cabinets, table and chairs. Nor had the farmer alluded to the falling man's gizzards, strewn across the Winkler gas range's grill, as if ready to be bar-b-qued and served up.

"Holy shit," exclaimed one of the federal agents.

"Land o'Goshen," stated Sheriff Tilley.

"Good Lord," whispered Gwen.

"What the fuck?" asked Agent Smith, then immediately regretted dropping the 'F' bomb. "I mean, holy cow," he quickly amended.

Who was the falling man? Whence did he arrive? And how came he to plummet through the Winkler home? Questions that needed answering.

But ten months after the FBI's forensic team had taken possession of body parts and clothing shreds, the identity of the falling man remained an enigma.

Not that there weren't a ton of clues, just none that might hint at a name of the deceased or a reason for him *being* deceased.

No wallet was found. Nor had the searchers uncovered a single bit of paper that might have helped ID the cadaver.

All his clothes were pure Walmart.

Neither his fingerprints nor his DNA showed up in any FBI database.

And because he hadn't a single filling or cap in the few teeth that were recovered, no dental records could be consulted.

A handful of skeletal remains were re-assembled and showed the man to be about six-foot five-inches tall. That notion was reinforced when a single Converse High Top shoe was found dangling from a Winkler rain gutter. It was a size fourteen and a half.

The FAA confirmed what Deputy Gwen had remarked to Sheriff Tilley: there was no regular commercial jet traffic in the skies north of Carrier.

And it proved impossible to learn from which airport a private plane might have taken off. Seems that Herschel, St. Marks, and Quintillion—the closest small airports—were all uncontrolled, meaning no towers, no one keeping tabs on comings or goings.

For the first few weeks after the body's discovery, print and electronic media reporters from around the globe had flocked to Carrier. Paparazzi hounded Sheriff Tilley and his deputy. The major networks and cable channels parked their news trucks hard by Morgan Winkler's barn. Many of their cameras were turned toward the heavens, the crews praying for an encore.

Winkler himself basked in his fifteen minutes of glory. BettyRae less so. Beau was kept hidden in his upstairs bedroom.

When the inquiry stalled, the media's interest flagged. They soon left Carrier and returned to covering Trump/Russia, an ongoing investigation now into its third year.

Neither the identity of the man, the reason for his earthward dive bomb, nor the aircraft from which he had jumped (been tossed? been ejected?) could be ascertained.

The case went cold.

That's not to say, however, that progress had not been achieved.

Deputy Gwen and Agent Smith began dating that very first night. She took the initiative and invited the diminutive fed to dinner at the Loma Alta.

After two weeks, they were going steady.

At the six-week mark, Agent Smith was heard to say that he had "a girl friend."

At four months, Deputy Gwen told her daddy she was in love. When her father learned that the object of her infatuation was a federal agent, *and* an Alabaman, to boot, the man began to froth. But his daughter would not be dissuaded.

At the seven month mark, the agent proposed and was promptly accepted.

The newly affianced couple thought it would be grand to be married at the Winkler farm on the anniversary of their meeting. A strange choice, many thought, but what the hell!

The morning of the nuptials broke warm and lightly breezy. Not a cloud in the sky. Most of Carrier was in attendance. Agent Smith's large family had traveled up from Tuscaloosa. Deputy Gwen's kin came from all across the Midwest.

The bride wore a dress sewn for her by BettyRae (after the entrance and exit holes in her sewing room were patched).

The groom looked resplendent in a white tux and elevator shoes that pushed him up to the five-and-a-half-foot mark.

They were married in the Winkler's flower strewn yard by the Rev. Carl Shelton (Food Hop Carl), the local Anabaptist lay preacher.

Rings, vows, and kisses were exchanged. The spareribs and corn-on-the-cob were devoured. The cake was cut and distributed.

Just as the bride and groom were about to begin the wedding waltz, a thunderous crash split the air, followed by a hailstorm of falling cedar splinters.

When the debris cleared, the celebrants turned to the Winkler home. On the south side of the roof there was a gaping, smoking hole.

And from a second story window, Beau was screaming, "It's happened agin. Only it be a lady this time."

#

Harry, Revealed

ROSENBERG SAT IN his kitchen having chicken noodle soup with matzo balls for lunch. From a Manischewitz jar, *nokh!*[1]

Since Frieda had run out on him, seven months earlier, Rosenberg had fallen on increasingly bitter times.

"Lunch ain't what it used to be," he thought. "Or life, neither," he added out loud to an empty kitchen.

The forty-three-year-old orthodox rabbi frowned at his microwave-heated meal and ran his fingers through his ample beard, chasing away assorted food droppings.

Rosenberg had always been a sloppy eater, going back to his days as a Talmudic student. Now things were much worse. His unkempt bush of a black beard and moustache totally engulfed his lips and acted as a barrier to solid food. The broth passed through easily enough, but a considerable amount of chicken, matzo ball, and carrot pieces never even got close to his mouth. They collected in the rabbi's beard and remained there until combed out after the meal. Or fell onto his lap. Or dropped back into the man's bowl for a second go-around.

It was a totally depressing spectacle that had, in no small way, contributed to the flight from their home of Frieda Kaplan Rosenberg, nineteen years and one daughter after her arranged marriage in Crown Heights to Harry, the handsome young rabbi.

Rosenberg recalled their courtship with mixed emotions. It had taken less than a month for the bloom to come off the marriage-rose.

---

[1] nokh: an all-purpose Yiddish word with a variety of meanings, depending on situation, intonation, etc. Here it means, broadly: "What kind of Jew eats store-boughten matzo ball soup?"

Frieda turned out to be a *shrai-er*[2] and took every opportunity to express, in no uncertain terms and with ever-increasing volume and vexation, her unhappiness with their marriage. Over the years, Frieda's complaints to her sister, Pearl, became more pointed.

"I shoulda married Alex Schatz, the diamond cutter," Frieda whined. "Or Sandy Mendelssohn, the plumber. Nothing but money from those two. But 'no.' I had to go marry a rabbi. What was I thinking?"

Frieda's disenchantment with her husband found its focus in a constant, biting critique of his table etiquette. "For G-d's sake, Harry," she'd shrai, "cut that ridiculous growth down to a manageable length and eat like a *mensch*.[3]"

Rosenberg good-naturedly had learned to endure his wife's relentless broadsides, never imagining them anything beyond what he, himself, had experienced growing up. Screaming and complaining, he believed, were for some Jews a bona fide mode of expression. Frieda was obviously one of that ilk. Their daughter, Rachel, the light of the rabbi's life, was not. Of course she had her own *meshugas*[4] he admitted to himself. But shrai-ing, happily, was not one of them.

Frieda's unanticipated flight from the Rosenberg home had a certain *b'shert*[5] element to it. Here are the details.

---

[2] shrai: while Gentile women may carry on and yell and occasionally even scream, many Jewish women, especially married Jewish women, shrai, a kind of vicious, menacing, cut-you-to-the-bone rant to which there is no known (legal) male response.

[3] mensch: literally a man, but in Yiddish, a decent and upright human being.

[4] meshugas: craziness. We all got our own.

[5] b'shert: fated, preordained

Jacobs, Rosenberg's regular *mohel*[6], had to go to Baltimore to be with his dying Aunt Millie. Normally not a particularly attentive family man, Jacobs told Rosenberg that since he was in line for a sweet pot of money from the ninety-six-year-old woman, he thought it behooved him to put in an appearance.

In his absence—which was scheduled for four days but lasted more than three weeks while Aunt Millie debated staying or leaving — twin boys were born in Rosenberg's East Flatbush parish. For the parents—Esty and Yankele Dishman —these were their sixth and seventh children in eight years of marriage. (The Dishmans bred like true *chasids*,[7] knocking them out almost one-a-year).

Rosenberg harbored a secret jealousy of the couple. Before he married, he had assumed that Frieda was like most orthodox Jewish women who took to heart the biblical admonition, 'Be fruitful and multiply.' But after the birth of Rachel, the rabbi's wife unilaterally called a halt to further pregnancies. No amount of coaxing or begging could move her. Rosenberg's dream—growing old as the father of a large brood of children—was dashed on the shoals of his wife's stubborn resistance.

Three days after the birth of the Dishman twins, the

[6] mohel: official, paid circumciser. And you thought being a proctologist was a weird job.

[7] Chasids: super-orthodox Jews who have organized themselves into a variety of sects, each following the teachings of particular rabbis—Lubavitch, Satmar, and Bobov being some of the better known groups. They wear dark black clothes, even in the heat of summer. They know everything, so don't try arguing with them. And they breed like rabbits. In Israel, Chasids generally don't recognize the government, resist serving in the army or paying taxes, but demand ever-larger federal subsidies for their state supported schools. Talk about chutzpah!

happy parents looked to Rosenberg to organize the *bris*.[8]

With Jacobs still away attending to Aunt Millie, Rosenberg phoned a colleague from the theological seminary.

"Krantz, darling. It's Rosenberg. I need a mohel."

"My G-d, Rosenberg. If you haven't had your *putz*[9] trimmed by now, I suggest you put the idea totally out of your mind. I hear it's way too painful at your age."

"You silly. I got twins that need cutting. Jacobs is away. You got, maybe, someone for me?"

"Well . . . I guess I can let you have Hochman. Came here two years ago from Jerusalem on a bogus visa, but the Lubavitchers pulled strings and he got to stay. He's a first class cutter. You'll like him. Better even, your twins'll like him."

Hochman arrived the day before the big event. He was set to overnight in Rachel's room, she having just left to go upstate to the Catskills to work as a youth director at Camp Abraham Stern.

The substitute mohel was a gaunt, morose man with sunken, nervous, deep blue eyes, teensy ears, a nose you could open a can with, a shock of unruly jet black hair, and the most seductively beautiful speaking voice anyone had ever heard.

Rosenberg was away at the synagogue when the mohel arrived. Frieda opened the door.

"I'm Hochman. The mohel."

Frieda stared. "Would you please say that again," she managed to whisper. "I'm not sure I heard you."

---

[8] bris: short for brit milah, or ritual of the covenant of circumcision. Big deal, big party. Held around the eighth day after the birth of a boy, usually on Shabbat.

[9] putz: penis

"I'm Hochman. The mohel," Hochman repeated in his beautiful baritone, standing rigidly on the porch, nervously twisting his black hat, his hair sticking out in a million directions.

Frieda stood in the doorway *and* at the crossroads. Tradition demanded that she not allow herself to be alone with the man.

But lo, the woman stepped back and motioned for him to enter. The mohel hesitated, trying to see past her. Perhaps the rabbi was out of view, Hochman thought. He reluctantly crossed the threshold and quickly scanned the room. His blue eyes bulged almost out of their sockets. *He was alone with the rabbi's wife!*

Frieda and Hochman faced each other in the center of the living room. He fidgeted, pulling at his beard, his eyes darting back and forth. She fidgeted, licking her lips and continually wiping her hands on her apron. Then, without fully realizing what she was doing, Frieda again broke with tradition: *she reached out her hand to the mohel!*

After an adult lifetime of neither touching nor being touched by any man (except by Rosenberg. But that, she often told her sister, "she could take or leave") all Frieda wanted to do now was feel Hochman's flesh. The mohel stared at the outstretched hand, realizing the immense implications of him taking it. Frieda took a step forward. Hochman blinked his gorgeous blue eyes at the rabbi's wife, and before you could say *mazel tov . . . .*

The bris went off next day at noon without a hitch. The twins, Charny and Abie Dishman, fussed a bit, but Hochman had a deft touch—the boys never knew what hit 'em. After receiving thanks and payment, the mohel disappeared.

Rosenberg stayed for the festivities and returned home about six that evening. In the kitchen, he found a note propped up next to a plate of cold chicken and boiled potatoes. "I'm gone forever. Don't try to find me," is all it said.

"*Gevalt!*[10] Rosenberg roared, casting his arms heavenward and tearing at his thick hair. He stomped around the kitchen, opening and slamming cabinet doors, banging his head against the wall, all the while shouting, "*shanda, shanda.*"[11]

Finally, exhausted, the rabbi collapsed into a chair next to the table, dropped his head onto his arms, and implored G-d to strike him dead. After an hour, his prayers unanswered (*So what else is new?*), Rosenberg raised himself up, saw the plate of food and reached for a drumstick. He tried to take a bite out of the chicken leg, but his beard got in the way.

Things went from awful to rotten for the newly abandoned rabbi. Within two days of Frieda's departure, Moskowitz, the bookie, showed up with a fist full of IOUs. It seemed Frieda had been playing the ponies for years. And lost. With unerring consistency.

Moskowitz at first apologized to Rosenberg, telling him that he never before had to collect from a rabbi. But business being business . . . .

Rosenberg was indignant and reminded the bookie of their G-d of Loving Forgiveness. "Didn't He send the angel to prevent Abraham from killing his own son?" the rabbi asked the bookie.

---

[10] gevalt: "Can this really be happening to me?"

[11] shanda: disgrace.

Moskowitz "tsked tsked" and responded by citing the Mosaic Law, "An eye for an eye," he intoned with finality, wagging his finger in the debtor's face.

Rosenberg didn't at all see the relevance and shot back with Rabbi Hillel's admonition about "doing unto others."

Never a big fan of the first century sage, Moskowitz remained unmoved and quoted to Rosenberg what he supposed was the appropriate Judaic rejoinder, *"The fathers ate boser.* [14] *The sons' teeth will be set on edge."*

Rosenberg wanted to argue that this analogy, too, was not apt. But the size of the truncheon the bookie now drew out of his umbrella convinced the rabbi to withhold further exegesis. After the two men concluded a payment schedule, Moskowitz agreed to take a glass-tea with the now tractable Rosenberg.

The rabbi's misfortunes were compounded the next day when someone named Zeitlin at Camp Abraham Stern called and asked where Rachel was.

"What am I hearing? You mean my daughter's not at camp?" the rabbi croaked, fear clutching at his throat.

"Never showed up," Zeitlin answered.

This bombshell drove the father crazy with worry. He spent the next two days calling all of his daughter's friends, finally tracking the wayward girl to Canarsie, where Rachel was "staying at Tony's."

Rosenberg's heart leapt into his mouth. He could hardly draw a breath. What were the odds that a pair of Italian Jews, maybe even from the Rome Ghetto, had, in a fit of misguided

---

[12] boser: a mysterious biblical food that was, and probably still is, bad for your teeth. Its deleterious effects are visited upon the children. So watch yourself!

joy, named their son Anthony? And then emigrated to Canarsie?

"Rachel darling. Who is this Tony person?" the rabbi was able to get out over the phone.

"An Italian boy, dad. His father owns a chain of pizzerias. But don't worry. He's circumcised. I checked."

Rosenberg fainted dead away. When he revived, an hour later, the enormity of his life's failures began to close in on him.

He tried prayer, but that hadn't worked for the man since seminary. In the middle of the winter of 1987, he had prayed for a snowfall of such severity that his Aramaic final, set for the next morning, might be cancelled.

"Biggest storm since 1914," the weatherman announced on the eve of the exam.

That was the first, last, and only time prayer had done the trick for Rosenberg. Lately he just crossed his fingers and hoped for a lucky break.

Over the next several weeks, the rabbi's attendance at Congregation B'nei Begin—his temple—became erratic. He claimed illness, but the congregants were no fools. Word about Frieda and Rachel had gotten around. Pretty soon, attendance began to dwindle, with many of the temple's younger parishioners abandoning ship, including the Dishmans. Many of the disenchanted migrated over to *Sha'are Tikva*,[13] the Reform temple around the corner. All Rosenberg knew about that shul,[14] ("...the one I wouldn't be caught dead in," he had once told Krantz) and all he needed to know, was that they

---

[13] Sha'are Tikva: Gates of Hope

[14] shul: synagogue, temple

sang. They had a *choir.* The cantor was a *woman. And* she played the guitar, *nokh.*[15]

Finally, one Friday afternoon, Rosenberg hit bottom. Sitting alone in his kitchen and drawing a total blank about what to say at that evening's services, he finished off half a bottle of homemade plum brandy. A few hours later, on the *bimah*[18], the rabbi slurred his way through the Torah reading.

"T'night's part is when Moses gets the tablets," he announced. "Ts'in the desert." He paused a moment, then brightened. "Sinai." Rosenberg gazed out into the almost empty shul. He leaned both arms on the lectern and grinned.

"I was there once. In '83," he confided deliciously. "Spent eight days on a nature trek. Me and Cynthia Isenberg. Fab'lus time. Eight days. Cindi 'n me." He stared at the twenty or so of the stunned faithful and smiled benignly at each one in turn. But in the front row, there was a new face—a severe, definitely hostile face.

His name was Malinovsky and his signature at the bottom of a letter to the temple's board of directors, copied to Rosenberg, made the beleaguered rabbi start to seriously graze his beard.

Malinovsky had written that, up until last Friday night's service ("Moses gets the tablets"), he and his family of sixteen had had every intention of joining the synagogue. But they were no longer interested, he wrote, due to the rabbi's obvious shortcomings.

Rosenberg paused in his reading, grinding his canines.

[15] nokh: Here is that word again, but in this sense, "Is that the craziest thing you ever heard? Having a woman play the guitar in temple? A shanda of the first magnitude!"

[16] bimah: raised stage in front of the congregation

The interfering *trombenik*[17] went on to caution that the glaring lack of attendance at services "should make it obvious to the board that there is trouble in the pulpit, and if that trouble was not addressed, the end of this synagogue's activities could not be far off."

The next day, Fritsch, the chairman of the temple's board, came to see Rosenberg.

"So Harry, tell me what's new by you," Fritsch began, affably enough.

Rosenberg wasn't taken in for a minute by the chairman's friendly opening. Fritsch was a wolf. A viper. Worse. A vulture. From the first, the two had their problems. But deception now seemed a false path to Rosenberg. He resolved to come clean. What the hell!

"Not so good, Morris. My life seems to have gone to shit. Frieda's living with Hochman the mohel. Rachel's living with Tony the Goy. And me? I'm hardly living at all. *Gutinyu*[18]."

"That's exactly what I wanted to talk to you about, Harry," the chairman of the board said in what Rosenberg thought was an ominously decisive tone.

On his fifth visit to see Mrs. Colleen O'Malley, his assigned employment officer, Rosenberg was ready to cash it in.

"So what I am hearing from you, dear lady, is that there are absolutely no jobs for an unemployed rabbi. Correct me if I am wrong."

The blue haired Mrs. O'Malley nodded with much

---

[17] trombenik: bum

[18] gutinyu: "If this isn't the end of the world, you could fool me."

practiced sympathy. "I'm afraid that's pretty much it, Rabbi Rosenberg. I tried to tell you at our first meeting, four months ago, that in all of my twenty-seven years with Employment Services, I've not received *a single* request from a synagogue looking for a rabbi. My suggestion is that you consider being re-trained."

"Marvelous," said Rosenberg, throwing up his hands. "I might try becoming a knockwurst stuffer for Oscar Mayer, or serving up hamburgers and ice cream on Saturdays at the local Wendy's."

Mrs. O'Malley nodded her agreement. "Either of those employment opportunities might work for you, Rabbi Rosenberg," she said sweetly.

If his family life and work were in tatters, Rosenberg's financial situation was also a train wreck. His monthly retirement was all but eaten up by his payments to Moskowitz, the bookie, for Frieda's debts. The truncheon, once seen, was not forgotten.

And now Rachel was beginning to sound serious about her Tony. What that meant, at a minimum, was $60,000 for wedding and dowry.

Over coffee at Mendy's Restaurant, on Avenue J in Flatbush, Rosenberg and Krantz caught up. The rabbi was surprised to learn that his wife and her mohel-lover were considering going off to the Argentine hinterlands to open a shul.

"They got Yids on the pampas?" Rosenberg questioned.

"Maybe some Jewish gauchos," Krantz speculated.

Rosenberg settled into a dark funk. "Krantz. I'm near the end of the line. I need a job."

The silence that greeted Rosenberg's plea caused the unemployed rabbi no little anguish. After a few minutes and without a great deal of enthusiasm, Krantz said, "Let me think on it for a day or two."

Her name was Dvora Silverman. She was a sweet-faced, twenty-two-year-old devout young woman, daughter, granddaughter and great-granddaughter of rabbis. Her knowledge of the Torah was the equal of any Talmudic student in her Bronx neighborhood. According to her parents, Solomon and Rivka, the young woman played piano like Horowitz and sang like Sills. She also cooked gefilte fish that made grown men weep. And she weighed in at approximately three hundred and seven pounds, making the prospects of finding her a husband daunting.

Enter Rosenberg in his new job: s*hadchan*.[19]

The rabbi was no stranger to the mysteries of matchmaking. Hadn't his own marriage to Frieda been arranged by Fanya the Far Seeing, the most famous and successful matchmaker in all of Crown Heights? The fact that Fanya had buried her first six husbands and was currently keeping an irregular death-watch at the bed-side of number seven (suffering from an intestinal disturbance the doctors at Cedars-Sinai were finding impossible to treat, let alone name) did in no way diminish her reputation.

When Fanya had first presented the shy and demure Frieda to Rosenberg—almost twenty years ago now—there had been no hint of a troubled future. But after their highly chaperoned, first meeting at Friday night services, Rosenberg

---

[19] shadchan: matchmaker

began to feel nervous. An indefinable scratching began to gnaw at his brain. *"Not the one, Harry. Not the one. Bail while you got the chance,"* it kept repeating. When he confessed his reservations to Fanya, she rushed to assure him it was typical of the betrothed to feel doubt.

Twenty years later, Rosenberg now fully appreciated the chanciness of matchmaking. He only hoped that the oft-married Fanya, now eighty-four and living on the top two floors of a Central Park West high rise, would some day realize the torture she had visited upon him.

The instant Rosenberg met Dvora, the matchmaker knew he had his work cut out for him, especially after the first eight prospects he arranged outrightly rejected the young woman based strictly on *hearsay*. It was clear to the rabbi he'd have to be creative. He searched far and wide for a groom.

In Coral Gables, Florida, Rosenberg found Dov Ostrovsky, a 45-year-old blind cantor from the *Reform*[20] Movement. He was a widower with four boys under fifteen, and an incontinent mother to care for.

"Not kosher enough," argued Solomon, Dvora's father.

"Lousy voice," pooh poohed mother Rivka.

"No way I'm cooking for that crew," said Dvora.

Rosenberg then suggested Brigham Shapiro, a

---

[20] Reform Movement: in Judaism, as in every religion, there are many gradations in the observance of the Deity: there are the ultra-observant, who can easily spend every waking hour in contemplation of the Holy One; the very observant, who might attend services daily, but reserve the bulk of their day for business and pleasure; the moderately observant who, if they are not scheduled to go to the Hamptons on the weekend, will come to Friday night services; the occasionally observant, who need to be dragged to services even when they have nothing better to do; and the non-observant, who aren't sure what the Torah is. The Reform Movement are the moderate guys.

seventeen-year-old convert to Judaism from Salt Lake City who professed a deep and abiding belief in polygamy.

"What the hell you trying to pull, Rosenberg?" Solomon demanded.

"Cut the crap," cautioned Rivka.

"Share the conjugal bed? Not me, buddy," haha-ed Dvora.

It took the best part of a month, but Rosenberg thought he hit pay dirt when he offered up Hyman Cohen, a seven foot, one inch, one hundred and sixty pound circus performer from Nova Scotia, discovered by the matchmaker on the 'Famous Jews of Eastern Canada' website.

Billing himself as 'Hymie the High-Flying,' the sixty-two-year-old trapeze artist admitted that the last time he had been in shul was for his own bris. Remarkably, he claims a memory of the event.

"Come up with someone or I'm gonna kick your ass," Solomon threatened.

"You got exactly one more chance, Rosenberg," Rivka warned.

Dvora looked daggers at the rabbi.

Down to his last shot, the desperate matchmaker dug deep . . . and was rewarded.

Chaim ben Kadari, a thirty-one-year-old, newly ordained rabbi was Rosenberg's most promising prospect. Originally from the village of Gori, in Soviet Georgia (Stalin's home town, a fact Rosenberg kept to himself), the groom-to-be was currently living in Kiev but was due in America in December to attend his cousin's wedding in Weehawken. Rosenberg saw his chance and grabbed it. Arrangements were hastily put together to *first* join Chaim and Dvora under the *chupah*[21] and *then* procure for the groom the highly sought after green card. The Lubavitchers' immigration experts were brought in as consultants.

Photos (head shots only) were emailed back and forth. Airline tickets purchased. Vows exchanged. Promises sanctified. The *kituba*[22] signed. The dowry settled. Chopped liver ordered.

Unfortunately, Chaim ben Kadari's name showed up on a Department of Homeland Security 'watch list,' so that within forty-five minutes of arriving at JFK, the young man was hooded, trussed, fettered, and tossed like a sack of Ukrainian potatoes into a CIA Gulfstream jet that rendered him to an unidentified, yet friendly (sic) Middle Eastern country for interrogation. The Lubavitchers were prevailed upon to use their international network of snoops, but so far, the whereabouts of Dvora's intended remains unknown.

Rosenberg and Krantz sat opposite each other in Mendy's. The mood was grim.

"What am I gonna do, Krantz?" the rabbi sobbed. "I can't go on this way. Look at me. I'm skin and bones. They're making a *luftmensch*[23] out of me."

"Calm yourself Rosenberg. I got a friend in Brighton Beach. Let me make a call."

Three days later Rosenberg was up to his shins in lamb guts and chicken blood.

The place was a huge South Brooklyn kosher butchery

---

[21] chupah: the wedding canopy

[22] kituba: the marriage contract

[23] luftmensch: literally 'air man,' someone who is so poor, he is sustained by air alone.

used by the Tomashevski crime family—late of Odessa—as a money-laundering front for their extensive illegal activities.

Kolya, the Tomashevski patriarch who had hired Rosenberg as a favor to Krantz, was a sweet old man of advanced years. The *capo* was reputed to have strangled with his own hands five members of a competing gang. Rosenberg didn't want to believe it.

The rabbi's job at the butchery was simple. After dispatching and bleeding the animals according to a tradition dating back millennia, the *shoichet*[24] would then affix his signature to a document certifying that the food was 'Kosher' and thereby fit for observant Jews around the world.

Although the *official* salary was much less than modest, the job was, in reality, an extremely well paying sinecure . . . if you knew the ropes. Because in many such facilities around the world, the attending rabbi can earn a very comfortable living by extorting kick-backs from food company owners. Rather than strictly observing the very onerous rules governing what's kosher and what's not, the owners *shtupp*[25] the rabbi and sweep the burdensome laws under the rug.

Old man Tomashevski had played the game forever—in the Old World and in the New—and had every expectation that he'd have to shtupp his new hire.

For Rosenberg, however, an honest-as-the-day-is-long naïf, participating in this centuries-old charade was beyond the pale. He took the work seriously . . . and paid for it. Or

---

[24] shoichet: ritual slaughterer, bound by long prescribed rules. It's what kosher meat is all about.

[25] shtupp: to stuff, but in this sense, to bribe. In another sense with the prefix 'unger' it means fabulously wealthy (literally, stuffed with money). And in a third, carnal sense, it means....well, you get the idea.

more to the point, *didn't* get paid for it. Because by the end of the first, seventy-four hour week, the rabbi pocketed a grand total of $161.34.

A deflated Rosenberg went back to Krantz.

"They pay me *bupkes*[26]" moaned the rabbi. "*Gournisht.*[27] *On rye!* Plus, I don't think I can ever look at a drumstick again," Rosenberg sniffled. "What else you got for me?"

Krantz deliberated over his cheese blintz. "I got a friend . . . " he began.

"I think I heard that one before," Rosenberg butted in, his voice heavy with sarcasm.

Krantz acknowledged the barb with a smile. "No. No. Really. Guy I know has a brother-in-law, secretary of the board at Sha'are Tikva."

"The Reform shul?" Rosenberg thundered, aghast. "You want *me* to work for those *pishers*[28]?"

"You got maybe a better idea?" Krantz asked.

In preparation for the job interview, Rosenberg (on Krantz' insistence) shaved off his beard. It took the better part of an hour and it was the first time in over twenty-six years that the rabbi had seen his naked face. A clean-shaven Harry regarded himself in the mirror. "My G-d," he said. "I'm not a bad looking man!"

Helen Frumkin completely agreed with Rosenberg's assessment of his own good looks. The Director of Education at Sha'are Tikva was a forty-five-year-old widow with two

---

[26] bupkes: literally 'goat shit,' but much more commonly, 'nothing.'

[27] gournisht: 'nothing.' On rye? Still nothing.

[28] pishers: literally pee-ers, but here, people of very little worth.

grown children and a five bedroom, three-balcony apartment in Prospect Park. Her husband Stanley had dropped dead one evening three years earlier at the crap table at the Trump Taj Mahal in Atlantic City after making twenty-four straight passes. The casino sent the widow a check for her late husband's winnings—$302,388—and a note of modest regret signed by The Donald himself.

Helen looked across the desk at Rosenberg, who was smiling shyly and sipping at the cup of tea she had offered him.

"How is it, rabbi?"

"Excellent tea, Misses," Rosenberg said quietly. "Thank you, again."

"My pleasure rabbi," she said, smiling graciously at the man. "I've read your resume. It's impressive. But I'm only wondering if perhaps you're not *over*qualified to teach Hebrew to our elementary school children."

"Overqualified, Misses? Not at all. I could hardly think of a sweeter group of people to work with," the rabbi said. "I'm crazy for kids."

The following summer, back at Mendy's, Krantz and Rosenberg were enjoying plates of apple strudel.

"Nu, Rosenberg. Bring me up to date," Krantz said.

"Well. My Rachel's now Mrs. Anthony Bonaventura, of Queens. Tony, my son-in-law, turns out to be a living doll. He worships the ground my daughter walks on. His *unger shtupped*[29] parents—who are also salt of the earth, by the way—split their time between here and Sicily, so Tony

[29] unger shtupped: stuffed with money

manages all seventeen pizzerias. They're gonna open three more next year, in Yonkers. A gold mine. The kids are trying to get pregnant and if it's a boy, G-d willing, Tony's agreed to a bris. I've already alerted Jacobs."

Krantz nodded. "Lovely. Very nice. And what about Frieda?" he probed delicately.

Rosenberg allowed himself a small smile. "She sent Rachel a short note from a place in Argentina called Las Cruces, near the Andes. She wrote that she and Hochman are having a hard time. She said they were almost lynched by gauchos when Hochman took out his blade and wanted to demonstrate on a ram how he makes his living."

Krantz chuckled. "And your work at Sha'are Tikva? Tell."

"Well, it turns out, I'm a terrific Hebrew teacher. Everyone is pleased with my work. The children adore me. And would you believe it, Krantz? I go to services. They're actually not too bad. We sing. I have a wonderful voice. At least that's what Helen . . . Mrs. Frumkin says."

Rosenberg beamed across the table at his old friend, then put an entire forkful of strudel into his mouth. It all made it in, without a single, fallen crumb.

\#

Cross Town Buses

MY OLDER BROTHER Arnie was a beatnik. Not quite a Dharma Bums-nik, but an almost charter member of Los Angeles' avant-garde colony that got rolling in the late forties, early fifties. He joined up as a twenty year old, took a two-year break when the US Army sent him to Korea, then jumped back in with both feet and continued for a good decade to live a life of experimentation, investigation, and extension of the envelope. The naysayers of every age call this kind of deviation from the social norm 'self-indulgence' and 'self-absorption.' Not me. As Arnie's younger brother, I viewed his life style with stars in my eyes.

Arnie did everything that membership in *La Vie Boheme* required of him: went to coffee houses to discuss the Meaning Of It All, attended poetry recitals to hear Ferlinghetti and Ginsberg declaim their latest, listened to a ton of the newly developing, ultra-cool West Coast Jazz, read and swore by Burroughs and Kerouac, smoked loads of reefer, drank like a fish, shared the affection of scores of women, came and went from the house at all hours, and shunned most things that were commonplace and acceptable in society.

He did not, however, reject his family. Nor did we reject him. The opposite. He remained throughout his life a loving and beloved son and brother who also happened to fill a very crucial familial role: he was our joke teller, the one person who could be counted on to come home with the latest story—in those days, jokes seemed to circulate more widely than today—and to deliver it with the supreme confidence of a Berle or a Benny. All of our large family would listen with rapt attention while Arnie would spin the tale, usually leaving us in stitches and tears.

He told this joke some time in the early fifties. I'm proud to say I got it *right away*. Here it is in a very much shortened version.

> *A hipster gets a job driving a bus in Manhattan, working the late night shift. A drunk gets on the bus around one in the morning and asks the driver, "Cross town buses run all night?" The hipster-driver begins to snap his fingers and answers, "Doo-dah. Doo-dah."*

The ten of us who made up our extended family were all raised on classical music. Not one of us played an instrument, but we were all avid listeners. Packed into a small one-bedroom Los Angeles apartment near the La Brea Tar Pits, we listened almost exclusively to KFAC, the city's classical music station.

But Arnie branched out, and took me, the youngest in our large household, with him.

He introduced me to the music of Coleman Hawkins, Stan Kenton, Dave Brubeck, Gerry Mulligan, and Lionel Hampton, jazz immortals whose albums continue to grace my iPod, my iMac, and my CD collection. He took me to a Hollywood dive to see my first live jazz: Teddy Buckner, a Dixieland trumpeting legend. I was twelve. Like it was yesterday.

To say that Arnie burned the candle at both ends doesn't near begin to do justice to the luminous, nova-like quality of my brother's life. You'd have to slice the candle into at least quarters, then light all eight exposed wicks to approximate the brightness *and* the evanescence of Arnie's too-short time on the planet.

He understood the chances he was taking. His gravestone, writ with Pink Floyd's carefully chosen words, says it all.

'Shine On You Crazy Diamond!'

My brother was one of the most generous and, at the same time, one of the most selfish people I've ever known. Hard to reconcile the two in the same person. Impossible to know why these two flip-sided traits found such a comfortable home together in Arnie's persona.

He could never do enough for me, his kid brother. In 1966, When I was stranded and broke in Norway, he wired me money to fly home. Whenever I needed wheels, he'd walk me around the lot of his rent-a-car on Sunset Boulevard and wind up giving me the keys to the Mercedes 350 SL convertible or the Lincoln Town Car, mine for free as long as I was in LA. And he introduced me to some of the most gorgeous women I've ever known.

Arnie was exceedingly generous to our mother. He was the second of her four sons and her favorite. With good reason. He was more than a dutiful child. He was a doting one. When she needed to get out of the house for her sanity's sake, Arnie found work for her in his rent-a-car office. In her last years, when she needed to be looked after, he put her up in a beautiful cottage in back of his home in the San Fernando Valley and took wonderful care of her.

To his wife and to his kids, however, he seemed to me to be much less giving. He wasn't faithful for a minute to his wife and, though he sincerely loved his kids and never, as far as I know, was abusive in *any* way, he had very little energy for them.

All the time in the world for his birth family, but very little for his married one. Who can know why?

Arnie was in a private clinic receiving very good care when he died in 1991. The immediate cause of his death was pneumonia, not necessarily a fatal illness. What made it mortal for my brother was the enfeebled state his body and mind had fallen into following a fourth cocaine-induced stroke.

The first of the four, sometime in the early 1980s, brought about a loss of some motor function in his right hand and arm. He shrugged it off and continued snorting.

The second stroke, in 1985, worsened the condition in his arm and added a slight, permanent twist to his mouth.

Cocaine had hardly been my brother's only indulgence. Although he ultimately joined the ranks of society's lock-steppers—he married, helped a little to raise three kids, went to work every day—he never shucked off any of the vices he acquired during his Beat Generation, salad days. I don't know why anyone would have expected him to.

He continued to drink and smoke cigarettes. He ran around and kept awful hours. He rarely exercised. And besides cocaine, he did bushels of grass, along with the occasional hallucinogen.

And he ate Spam. A holdover from his days in the army. He might have survived the ersatz meat, but once cocaine was added to the mix, it was only a matter of time.

Not that Arnie loved cocaine all that much. It seemed to me, *at least in the beginning*, to be more of an affectation. That's what cool people do. They snort coke. And cool was what Arnie always wanted to be.

But cocaine is seductive. In the beginning it's one thing. Later, quite another, as he was to discover.

His rental car business brought him into daily contact with all kinds of cool people—the music and show biz crowd. They all wanted cocaine and my brother was there to supply them. It was good for his business. But even more, it allowed Arnie entrée into a world he coveted and needed: a glamorous life, women by the carload, front row seats at Laker games, rock concerts, rubbing elbows with the glitterati at Wolfgang Puck's.

After he separated from his wife, Arnie bought a large home in Laurel Canyon. He threw a party once when I was visiting LA. I came home to discover an open coke-bar upstairs with a two-pound mound of powder on a large slab of shiny black marble and an array of snorting tools nearby. People were coming and going, doing lines, doing spoons, helping themselves.

I went ballistic. I took him aside and warned him that anybody, any cop, might walk in and radically alter his life. He assured me that he had friends in high places, judges and lawyers who would protect him. I reminded him that just two weeks earlier, a buddy of his, one to whom Arnie had sold, had been arrested for cocaine possession-for-sale and might wind up naming my brother in order to cop a plea.

Arnie was grateful for my concern, but dismissive. "Never happen," quoth the maven.

A short week later, he was arrested in his office selling to an undercover agent. What's worse, my mother, who was there at the time, had to watch her beloved son cuffed, Mirandized, and escorted to the just-arrived squad car.

Needless to say, the "friends in high places" failed to

materialize. He got twenty-four months. A plea bargain was offered, but he had to name the higher ups, the people who had sold him cocaine by the kilo. The problem for my brother was that people who sell cocaine by the kilo usually have large guns and are not afraid to use them. While he considered the offer, the higher-ups got word to him that if he fingered them, they would kill him. Arnie never doubted they were serious, kept mum, and took his medicine.

My brother Dave and I visited him in prison, a minimum-security lock-up about four hours north of LA. Arnie looked surprisingly good. In shape, lean, healthy, somehow tanned. Best I had seen him look in years.

When he got out, he stopped trading in cocaine, but resumed snorting right away and continued until he could no longer lift the coke spoon to his nose.

Arnie's third stroke, around 1988, deepened his facial paralysis, slurred his speech, slowed his thought, and rendered most of the right side of his body effectively immobile. He needed a cane to get around. Still, he continued using.

One evening in a crowded restaurant, he brazenly pulled a tiny coke vial and spoon from his pocket and began to indulge right there and then. No one at our table, except me, seemed in the least bit incommoded by this outrageous act. I rose, began shouting, and threatened to leave unless he stopped. In deference to me and to the attention I was purposely attracting, he put the coke away. After dinner, however, on the way to our car, he couldn't resist.

The fourth stroke, in early 1990, reduced him to the vegetative state he was in when pneumonia finally put him down for the count. An apt metaphor. Because one of the crazier things my brother had tried as a teenager was amateur boxing. He wisely gave it up after getting his head handed to him in his first fight. There's a photo floating around the family archives of him in shorts, in a faux boxer pose.

That last stroke put him in an intensive care clinic and left him in an anomalous condition. He appeared alert. Could follow you with his eyes. Could sit up. But couldn't talk. Couldn't walk. Couldn't gesture. And saddest of all, couldn't let you know in *any* way that he understood *any*thing that was going on around him. He could raise his eyebrows and smile, but it was never clear whether it was in response to something I said or was simply an external reaction to some internal twinge.

I had flown in from Manhattan for a few days and visited with him twice in the clinic. The first time, I just hung out, making one-sided small talk, not knowing whether he understood me or not.

I went back the next day with a plan: I would read to him. I'm not sure what prompted me to do this, it just seemed appropriate. Perhaps it was more for my benefit than for his. I chose my favorite short story, *The Laughing Man*, the most touching and brilliant of J.D. Salinger's *Nine Stories*. It's a very New York tale and, in my mind, captures the spirit and wonder of youth better than anything I know. Arnie had read and loved all of Salinger's slim output, so I knew he had read *The Laughing Man*. All of our family are New Yorkers and I thought if something was going to get through to him, this quintessentially Gotham-in-the-1930s story might just stir a happy memory of his growing-up days in the Bronx.

I read it to him early one afternoon. It took about half an hour, maybe longer. I was clearly the more affected of the two of us. At the surprising and very sad ending of this bittersweet fable, I could barely read through my tears. Sitting up in his bed, Arnie had listened impassively, dry-eyed, looking at me the whole time, but never communicating or registering a single anything that showed he understood what I had read or what I was doing.

That was all of it. I gave him a long hug, kissed him goodbye, left the clinic, and flew home.

Arnie died two weeks later.

Though I no longer live in Manhattan, I visit regularly. Whenever I climb on board the M27 or M50 bus that shuttles back and forth across the island, eastside-westside, I always ask the driver, *"Cross town buses run all night?"*

So far, I haven't gotten the response I'd love to hear. But I hope to. Someday.

#

A God by Any Other Name

WHEN STATE UNIVERSITY'S first-string field goal kicker knelt down on the sidelines during the break between the third and fourth quarters of Friday night's game against the Broncos of West Valley, proceeded to unroll his prayer rug, then raised his arms heavenward and called out in a deeply pious voice that reverberated from goal post to goal post, "Allahu Akhbar," the preponderantly Christian crowd of 8,716 football fans packed into Crutcher Stadium smiled to each other and patted themselves on the back, self-congratulatorily: Yes, despite what those ACLU East Coast liberal-wonks might say, religious toleration was alive and well in America's heartland.

Because by this time, the sixth game of the most successful season ever enjoyed by the Red Coyotes of State U., the strictly observed evening prayer ritual of Tha'labah Ali Jinnah, exchange student from Rawalpindi, Pakistan, was well known, and occasionally even moderately celebrated throughout the Great Plains.

But it wasn't always like that. Unh-uh.

The first time Tha'labah had prayed to his God out loud on the football field came in the year's opener against the Wandering Bisons of Bullwarren A & G.

To say that the crowd at *that* game was taken aback by the surprise rug unfurling hardly begins to express the torrent of verbal outrage and vitriol that poured down from the bleachers. Catcalls and threats of the most vicious nature spilled from a thousand lips, denouncing the young man, his religion, and his God. Connections to 9/11, Osama bin Laden, ISIS, and Al Qaeda were hurled at Tha'labah as he bowed in devotional observance on his east-facing prayer rug, oblivious to the furor he was creating.

But football fans are nothing if not fickle.

Because when Tha'labah's forty-two yard, game winning field goal split the uprights as time expired, giving the Red Coyotes a one point win and their first victory against the Wandering Bisons since Bush the First asked the country to read his lips, most of the boos and jeers were forgotten and the new hero somewhat forgiven for not believing in the crowd's preferred deity.

After a second win against the Muskrats of Pawnee County, history then repeated itself in the Red Coyotes' third game against the College City Jay Hawkers when Tha'labah's fourth field goal in the last minute was the difference in State's 12-10 squeaker.

Now, with the young man's devotional duties having become a staple and *a crowd favorite*, a new and surprising element was injected into the Coyotes' fourth game against the Barley Huskers of Prairie City.

The real surprise, however, was the origin of this unexpected and fateful turn of events: State U's Greeks.

The frat boys from Gamma Omega Psi Epsilon Epsilon were regular attendees at all of the Red Coyotes' home games and were ardent followers of their new champion, whom they decided to honor just as Tha'labah began his regular between-quarters prayers. At that exact moment, the frat boys astonished the crowd by rising up, *en masse*, and waving improvised, mini-prayer rugs.

The object of their enthusiasm took it all humbly in stride, waving back to the Greeks and smiling his acknowledgment before kneeling down and invoking the Holy Spirit.

State won the game, by the way, in a blowout, 61-6, with Tha'labah kicking four field goals and adding seven extra points.

With most of his starters pulled from the game and resting, Coach Stanislav Grba decided to have some fun. "Tha'labah," he shouted down the bench. "Go be our quarterback for the next set of downs. Just hand off to the fullback. Nothin' fancy."

The young man, who harbored secret dreams of playing quarterback, did exactly as he was told and successfully handed off the ball three times, then floated back to the sidelines.

Coach Grba was pleased. "Way to play," the coach encouraged his newly discovered, fourth-string Q-B.

The Greeks continued waving their mini-prayer rugs at each of the next five games, all won by the Red Coyotes. Many in the crowd began to suspect a prayers-being-answered connection between State's unprecedented 9-0 record and the invocation of the Islamic Deity. Could it be?

Just before the team's final regular season game, the one they needed to win to earn a first-ever post-season bowl bid, fate stepped in and elevated the young man's heroics from the exceptional to the Olympian.

It began on Monday, when Beau Beauchamp, the squad's first-string quarterback, wrenched his knee playing hacky-sack with three sorority sisters from Nu Omega Sigma Epsilon Xi.

Then on Wednesday, Barton (The Hunk) Hankowski, the Coyotes back-up Q-B, cut off the tip of the pinky of his throwing hand while slicing into a kumquat.

And finally on Thursday morning (not totally unexpectedly, many fans would later tell the press), State's third string Q-B, Marvin (The Fly) Tsetserovsky was declared ineligible due to the discovery in his blood of trace quantities of MegaBod 4Bt, a human growth hormone which, over the course of the previous three months, had turned The Fly's 160 pound frame into a 225 pound Bondian, no-neck behemoth.

With his quarterback ranks thus depleted, there was nowhere else for Coach Grba to go.

"Tha'labah. You're it," the coach told his kicker at Thursday afternoon's practice. "You're gonna be our quarterback next week against Acton Falls. If we win, we'll be Ogallala Conference champs. Meaning, a post-season game, sump'en we ain't achieved in . . . well, I can't rightly 'member the last time. Are you with me, son?"

"I'll do my utmost, Coach Grba, insha'Allah," the newly promoted starting Q-B answered.

"Right," said his coach.

Had State only been experiencing one of its usual sub-.500 seasons, Tha'labah's elevation to first team might have gone mostly unremarked.

But because of the school's current winning streak, due in large part to the exchange student's perfect PAT count (27 out of 27 points after touchdowns) and impeccable field goal kicking (18 in a row, no misses, longest—56 yards) the revelation that a Pakistani, a Muslim, and a walk-on, no less, would be starting at Q-B for an American football team cruising toward the post-season drew the attention of the world-wide media.

The *Al Jazeera* Washington DC correspondent was rushed from covering the Ukraine whistle blower investigation and dispatched to report on the game. *Dawn*, the Pakistani English language daily, gave Tha'labah the front page: three pictures, six full columns, and an interview with his mother in Rawalpindi. And *Sports Illustrated* sent Hansel Carmoody, its Pulitzer Prize winning journalist, to cover the game for the magazine's winter swimsuit edition.

Because Crutcher Stadium's 9,000-seat capacity couldn't begin to satisfy the hordes of folk coming from all corners of the globe and demanding tickets to 'The Game,' the venue for State's showdown with the Spotted Heifers of Acton Falls had to be changed. The new site for the titanic contest was the 75,000 seat Corrigan Motor Speedway in Dermott, in the middle of the state. The venerable race track had earned its reputation in 1954 when it staged the largest demolition derby in automotive annals—1,762 cars destroyed.

In deference to the thousands of fans who were coming from abroad, many of them Muslims, the usual football ballyhoo (tail gate pork bar-be-ques, nearly naked cheerleaders) was dispensed with. What this crowd wanted was a game. And boy, did they get one!

The first half was a brutal defensive struggle that saw a total of seven first downs, five by the Heifers and only two by State. A single Acton field goal accounted for all of the scoring.

Which was fine with Coach Grba. Given the lack of experience of his new Q-B, the cautious coach had called only three passing plays the entire half. Tha'labah was thus consigned to handing the ball off to his running backs, none of whom, however, could gain more than a few yards per carry against a very stout Acton defense.

Things barely changed in the second half, so that by the end of the third quarter, only another Acton field goal showed on the scoreboard, giving the Spotted Heifers a 6-0 lead.

The eyes of all State fans now turned to Tha'labah, hoping that the young man's between-quarters prayers might show the way to the post-season.

With the chance of a bowl game in mind, State's frat boys had pulled out all the stops. With help from their Nu Omega sorority sisters, the Greeks had devised a special bit of encouragement: just as Tha'labah began unrolling his prayer rug, preparing to humble himself before his God, the Greek young men and women rose up: "Tha'labah-bow, Tha'labah-bow, Tha'labah-bow," they screamed, hoping to strengthen the young man's resolve and propel the Coyotes to victory. Their hero paused, turned toward the stands, smiled broadly, and then commenced to bow eastward, to honor Allah.

The chant continued for only half a minute before a problem arose. The young Pakistani's first name had never found a comfortable place on the tongues of his American hosts. And given the besotted state of affairs among the Greeks that evening (and most evenings, if truth be told), the chanters quickly fell out of cadence and the chant degenerated into something quite incoherent.

The Greek young men and women were up to the challenge, however. They improvised a huddle in the stands where they soon devised a simpler chant, one that they, the other folks in the stadium, and every Muslim on the planet soon grew to love. By judiciously shortening their star's first name, an elegant solution was devised.

"T-bow, T-bow, T-bow," the Greeks shouted, alternately standing and sitting in a wave and signaling joyfully with their mini-prayer rugs.

The cadence now simplified, the chant seemed to electrify the spectators and was taken up by all of State's fans.

"T-bow, T-bow, T-bow," State's partisans thundered,

joining the Greeks in wave after wave of unanimous support for their Pakistani-born star.

And, as if inspired by his fan base (and certainly by divine intervention, many in the stands felt) the young man, once again, lived up to the impossibly high expectations thrust upon him by a world desperate for true heroes.

With only seconds remaining, and trailing Acton 6-0, T-bow Jinnah delivered the goods: a fifty-five-yard Hail Mary that his right end, six-foot, ten-inch D'Andre Witherspoon Jr., leaped high to gather in at the one yard line, before falling into the end zone to tie the score.

The point after, child's play for the Red Coyote's superb place kicker, clinched the victory and sent State U. rocketing into the post-season.

The rest, as the saying goes, is history, the details of which we need not recount here. If you must, you can always go to Google.

Suffice it to say that the January 4th Stock Yard Bowl against the Green Tasers of South Bloomington Poly, was simply the finishing touch to a saga that has achieved epic status, both on the campus at State University and in Tha'labah's home town of Rawalpindi.

The modesty of the publicity-shy young man precluded the press from creating the media circus it would have so loved to visit upon him.

And despite immense monetary offers for interviews, our hero deigned to give only one, to *The Howler*, State's own paper.

That interview took place late one spring morning. The Pakistani exchange student told the reporter that he would be heading home after graduation and doubted whether he would return to America in the near future.

Just as the reporter was about to ask her next question, T-bow Jinnah looked at his watch, excused himself politely, left the building, and went out onto the lawn in front of *The Howler* offices. There, Tha'labah Ali Jinnah turned to the east, unfurled his prayer rug, and prepared for midday devotion.

#

Miranda Does Her Thing

WITH ELBOWS ON the table, palms cupping his face, Perry Colangelo, veteran writing workshop teacher, wondered if he had ever heard anything as mystifying and clumsy as the short story now being read aloud by its author, Ellie Jarvis, one of Perry's long-time students. Mercifully, the woman was coming to the end of her reading.

> *Cell phone pressed to her ear, Miranda listened with indifference as Carlos whispered in his husky voice, "Te amo, guapa. Te amo."*
>
> *Dressed only in the sheerest of teddies, Miranda lay back onto her silken sheets, her long legs reaching well beyond the end of the bed, her right hand loosely cradling the Samsung.*
>
> *"Ola, Miranda. Donde estas?" Carlos' pleading voice came through to her as if from a great distance. "You still there, guapa?"*
>
> *Miranda Davidson sighed once, rolled onto her stomach, then pushed the red button on her cell phone, disconnecting her ex-lover from her life, once and for all . . . and forever.*

Ellie Jarvis sat back, an enigmatic smile on her face as her teacher and five classmates strived mightily to contort *their* faces into expressions of modest approval.

It was Perry's unspoken policy in situations like this —so fraught with distressing, possibly even writing-career-ending remarks—to try and speak first, to set the tone, to say a few words of encouragement that might elicit similar positive comments from his students. This evening, however, in the face of such a bizarre and disjointed offering, Perry decided to keep his mouth shut, determined to let the literary chips fall where they might, preferably all over his student's maladroit effort.

Although he was paid per capita and needed every customer he could find, Perry was willing to bite the monetary bullet in hopes that Ellie Jarvis would *finally* become discouraged enough to discontinue her literary career and drop out of his class. Perry looked around the table. "Bill, why don't you start?"

Bill Dworsky, a twenty-six-year-old multi-pierced and tattooed mechanic from Red Hook, was among the most promising writing students with whom Perry had ever worked —a true diamond in the rough. The young man wrote biting satires about competing motorcycle gangs in the San Francisco Bay Area drug trade that exercised a breathtaking amount of violence against each other. Bill's current work, *Yamaha Hell, Harley Heaven,* was a total send-up: rival lesbian biker packs from Oakland are hired as crowd control at a Grateful Dead concert during 1967's *Summer of Love.* The situation becomes incendiary when Jerry Garcia puts the move on a member of the *She Wolves,* starting a tidal wave of events that culminates a month later at the Democratic Convention in Chicago, in the hotel room of Abie Hoffman.

Although Perry thought Bill a rather cavalier historian, the writing teacher believed the young man's work had flashes of very original wit and marvelously explicit sex.

Bill screwed up his face into a thoughtful expression.

"I liked it. I liked it that Miranda *finally* called Carlos' bluff." The young man looked around at his colleagues-in-prose and seemed gratified that a few eager nods returned his gaze. "I mean, the guy's been dickin' 'round forever, makin' promises, then breakin' 'em. I'm glad Miranda came to her senses and dumped him. I wish she woulda done it a long time ago. She don' need that low life. She's strong enough to make it on her own. So . . . I guess the story worked for me."

Bill was now able to relax, a look of relief passing over his face. He had done his part, had found something nice to say about Ellie Jarvis' literary debacle.

Perry jumped in. "Patti?"

Patti Ditmar was a forty-six-year-old assistant professor of music at Hunter College who wrote fantasy stories for *tweens*, stories that her writing teacher considered sophomoric and hackneyed. Patti's recent contribution to class (that drew from two of her colleagues the most dreaded of all criticism: "very interesting") was called *Tales of the Tundra*. It was the story of a young native boy in Alaska whose parents get eaten by a mountain lion named Qan-sher. The boy, Gli-mow, is adopted by a band of wolves and is raised thinking himself one of the pack. Along the way, Gli-mow is befriended by a large grizzly, Loo-ba, and a lynx, Heer-Baga. The three of them have one rollicking adventure after another until Gli-mow begins to feel a human longing for a young woman, Ne-Ja, whom he has espied in an Eskimo village. The story ends predictably with Gli-mow and Ne-Ja skipping off into the wild, trailed by their own helpful menagerie.

When a few members of the class noted the similarity of her story with both *The Jungle Book* and *Tarzan*, Patti, appropriately, went ape. She admitted having read both books "many, many, *many* years ago," but she vehemently denied any borrowing.

Perry, however, wasn't convinced and took each of the names in Patti's tale and flipped the syllables, revealing to her the main characters in Kipling's *and* Burroughs' classics. Patti burst into tears, allowing that "perhaps there *was* a similarity." She then fled class. Tonight's appearance marked her return after three weeks away.

Seeming none the worse for her absence, Patti jumped at the chance to challenge Bill's critique. She and the mechanic had hardly ever agreed during their time together in this 92nd Street Y writing class. Perry dates their troubles to an announcement Bill made several months earlier—that he just finished rebuilding a 1983 Harley Roadster and had celebrated by driving it into Manhattan for their class. Patti suggested that she'd "love to have a ride." When Bill politely demurred, the music teacher sank into a funk that over time had morphed into a full-fledged and constant bout of pique against Bill and his literary commentary.

"There you go again, Bill. But I have to disagree with you," she now began. "You've missed the point. As usual."

The rest of the group braced themselves for another edition of 'Patti skewers Bill.' But more to the moment, they all felt the heat temporarily off their *own* need to say something nice about Ellie's latest and most grotesque effort.

"I'm not sure you appreciated Carlos' sincerity," Patti threw out, the barest hint of snidely-put-down in her voice. "He gave Miranda exactly what she needed. He was always going the extra mile for her. But *she* kept pulling back. Listen to this great passage, Bill," Patti said, searching through her marked-up copy of *Miranda.* "Here it is."

"I give you everything, guapa. Everything I got. I never love no woman like I love you." Carlos pulled off his t-shirt, exposing his smoothly rippling pecs, a

perfect six-pack, and slightly sweaty, bronzed skin. His nipples were hard. He took a step toward her. "Why don'you see it? You think 'cause I steal cars for a living I can' love you like a real man?" Carlos cried out like a wounded lion, "You wrong, guapa. You wrong!"

"See, Bill," Patti said. "*He's* fully committed. But listen how *she* reacts."

Miranda insouciantly tossed her long, ash-blond tresses back over her creamy shoulders, covering her 'Born to be Free' tattoo.

"Oh Carlos, please," Miranda insisted. "We've been through all this before. It's not because we're from different cultures. It's simply . . ." Her voice trailed off while she stubbed out her cigarette in a potted ficus plant. "It's just that . . . Mexican food is far too spicy for me! If you get my drift."

Patti finished reading the passage and sat back triumphantly. "There it is Bill. Clear as day. Miranda's the loser in this one. And I, for one, am glad Carlos won't have to put up with her anymore." Patti looked around the table for support. An oil painting of deathless stares greeted her. Undismayed by the obvious inability of her colleagues to read literature with more discernment, Patti continued, now with more than a little sarcasm, "It's clear *to me*, Bill, that Miranda is getting *just what she deserves!* Just what any Stuck. Up. *Bitch*. Deserves."

Dorothy Chen, an elderly retired social worker and a relative newcomer to the writing workshop, clasped her hands together in her lap, tucked her head into her shoulders and pulled herself deep into her chair.

Oblivious to her classmate's discomfort, Patti plowed on, "Miranda never appreciated what Carlos was offering her —a chance to see life as it *really* might be lived. Isn't that what *you* had in mind, Ellie?"

All eyes now swiveled to the author of *Miranda Does Her Thing,* the twenty-four page short story Ellie Jarvis discovered in her apartment soon after awakening from a hallucinogenic la-la-land stupor that had extended over most of the Memorial Day weekend. Ellie *believes* she wrote it, but is not one hundred percent certain. What she *is* certain of is that she must never reveal to her classmates that the probable inspiration for this latter-day *Kubla Khan* was found in eight large peyote buttons her boyfriend, Manny Orozco, brought back from a trip to his home pueblo, close to Taos, New Mexico.

Ellie now flashed back to Manny opening up the small, buckskin pouch and spilling the peyote out onto her kitchen table. He had set about cleaning the buttons as carefully as he could, assuring Ellie that he would cut out all those poisonous little nodes which, if ingested, invariably cause a bout of nausea and vomiting prior to the fabulous and legendary onset of peyote psychedelia.

Unfortunately, Manny didn't do the job as well as he might have and, despite the Oster-blended fruit smoothie that he prepared to get the vile tasting peyote past the palate and down the gullet, they both had to suffer through a short but intense round of "barking Europe at the toilet," as Manny laughingly referred to it. Only then were they able to begin the "grooviest, most far out trip" he and Ellie had ever experienced.

For reasons best understood by the Gods of Hyper-consciousness, Ellie and Manny did *not* have sex while under the influence—the first instance of drug-induced *abstinence* either could remember. "We just said 'no,'" Ellie told her sister later. "And it was totally cool."

Instead of sex, each had sought out a corner of Ellie's small one bedroom apartment on East 18th, and, in her words, "We just did our own thing."

In Manny's case, it was interpreting ancient Hopi dances. Dressed only in a leather loincloth, deer skin moccasins (fashioned by his blind shaman uncle), sea shells anklets (an Aztec affectation, he later admitted) and the traditional Hopi turquoise and beaten silver bracelets around wrists and biceps, Manny danced to his own singing and drumming for sixteen straight hours. He then wolfed down an entire pint container of prawns with Chinese broccoli, drank a liter of warm Dr. Pepper, and collapsed onto their bed, not moving a muscle until the next evening.

Later, when he asked about *her* trip, Ellie had trouble remembering. The only thing she had to show for the experience was *Miranda Does Her Thing,* which she discovered next to her computer in a pile of neatly printed and numbered pages, 12 point Times New Roman. And spell-checked.

She told Manny she wrote it, *she thinks*, as a stream-of-memory recounting of a story she either heard *from* Miranda Winterbottom, or perhaps heard *about* Miranda Winterbottom, she being an obscenely wealthy young woman with absolutely no brains and an enormous nose who received a legacy acceptance to Columbia and was Ellie's roommate for their first year there. Ellie told Manny later that she "hadn't thought of Miranda even one time since she packed up her nose and moved out of their dorm," transferring to the west coast, to USC.

The author, of course, had no intention of sharing with the group the details of her drug-induced composing frenzy. After all, she thought, Coleridge almost certainly didn't confide in Wordsworth.

She told her classmates, rather, it was an older piece. "I wrote it years ago while in college, dug it out, and wanted to workshop it now for the first time."

"Great," said Patti enthusiastically. "But what did you have in mind for the ending? I mean, who do *you* see as the hero of your story?"

Challenged for the first time to explain why thirty-seven-year-old Miranda Davidson, the jet-setting heiress to the Tabby Cat Litter millions, should have fallen in love with eighteen-year-old Carlos Moreno, an illiterate, illegal alien working in an East L.A. chop shop, a clueless Ellie Jarvis sought escape and lobbed the question to the other side of the table.

"What do *you* think, Perry?" Ellie asked her writing teacher as playfully as she could. "Who do *you* feel comes out on top?"

Perry Colangelo now came suddenly alert and sat up straight. He had hoped he might be freed from the need to express an opinion. Apparently, that was not to be. As he cleared his throat, he was caught up suddenly in an epiphanous moment: he realized that in all of his sixteen years of conducting these workshops he had never once told a student that her or his writing stunk. Would this be the first time? Why not, he thought? Why not simply tell Ellie—as nicely, calmly and sweetly as he could—that perhaps she should re-think returning for the next semester?

Perry now began recalling bits and pieces of Ellie's past several efforts, all of which he thought he had successfully erased from his memory. But there they were again: *George Bites Mary,* a Dracula spoof set in Timbuktu during the Barbary Wars; *Ever Stepped in Gunk?* a love story involving two Australian aboriginals with Tourette's Syndrome; and *Lou and Andy,* a 'what-if' two act play chronicling a chance sexual encounter in the Pyrenees between Louise Bourgeois and Andy Warhol.

But before Perry could take that fateful step, he was saved—a cell phone began jangling. A deeply embarrassed Dorothy Chen fumbled through her purse until she found the offending device and shut it down, all the while apologizing profusely to the group.

The aged Chinese woman was a favorite student of Perry's. She wrote travel and cook books focusing on the landscape and cuisine of certain valleys along the Yangtze River.

Soon after Dorothy joined the class, Perry learned on Google that China's spectacular environmental boondoggle, the Three Gorges Dam, had flooded *all* of the places mentioned in her books, thereby rendering site-seeing impossible (except by glass bottomed boat) and all of the recipes using locally grown foods uncookable. Perry wasn't sure Dorothy realized this and hadn't the heart to tell her.

Now, however, he was more than happy to use her cell phone's interruption as a way to relieve himself of the onerous duty of commenting on *Miranda.* He thought it totally appropriate to bounce the question over to Dorothy. After all, he reasoned, he was the teacher and could damn well do whatever he wanted in *his* class. A stolen glance at the wall clock told him he could legitimately call an end to this torture in ten minutes.

"Dorothy, why don't *you* chime in," Perry said. "Who do *you* think ends up better off, Carlos or Miranda?"

Dorothy stared back at Perry with what he imagined was as malevolent a look as this lovely older woman could conjure. She took a deep breath and began slowly, carefully weighing each word.

"I liked many parts of this story, Ellie, dear. The time when Miranda goes with Carlos to the parking lot at Dodger Stadium to steal antennas and DVD players. That was very suspenseful. And when the two of them swam naked in the surf at Malibu among the jellyfish during the thunder and lightning storm. That was thrilling. And then when Carlos met her father and Miranda pretended that the gentleman was her former lover, that was very amusing. But, I have to tell you, my dear, there were many unanswered questions for me."

"For me, too," another student now eagerly agreed.

The new voice belonged to Cassi Harcourt, a very short, thirty-year-old woman from Virginia who at one time trained horses for a living and had the distinction in this class of actually finishing a novel through three drafts. She calls the book *Wanda the Wonder Horse*, which she described in the query letter the other students helped her prepare as "a dressage-based mystery in which a thirty-year-old woman jockey/trainer from Virginia takes her New York policeman/ boyfriend's horse to the Olympic Equestrian Trials in Daytona Beach."

Over the past couple of years, Perry and a slew of writing students have nursed Cassi through the myriad technical obstacles posed by the twenty-two major characters in this labyrinthine Gotham-oater-mystery.

The novel's most daunting moment occurs the week before the Olympic Trials when Wanda gets spooked in the line of duty during a Central Park, *Free Tibet* rally. Things get ugly when a crazed Buddhist monk tosses a bunch of lit firecrackers directly under Wanda. The traumatized animal rears up, throwing the equestrian cop/boyfriend to the ground where he lies unconscious as hundreds of chanting, saffron-robed Tibetans use his body as the center piece for a hastily improvised mandala. Happily, both cop and horse recover in time for the trials.

Cassi now looked at Ellie and nodded. "I agree with Dorothy," she began. "That part in the surf was cool but when they came out of the water and a bolt of lightning struck the lifeguard station, setting it on fire, I didn't get that part. And then they were out on the beach all night while Miranda whistled *Singin' in the Rain*? That just didn't seem to fit in with the rest of the story. It didn't make any sense. Know what I mean?"

Ellie looked mutely at Cassi, having zero recollection of that particular scene. Her tentative smile not finding a sympathetic echo from the less than friendly group of faces that sat regarding her, Ellie kept mum.

Wanting in no way, shape, or form to take the floor from his students, Perry tried to keep the leaden ball of criticism rolling. "Al. Want to finish up?"

Allesandro Lanza, a squat, always nattily attired mid-fifty-ish barber from Hell's Kitchen wrote syrupy bi-lingual stories about Italian life in the Lower East Side during Fiorello La Guardia's three terms as mayor of New York City.

Lanza was perhaps the most picayune critic Perry had ever had in any class. The Italian-American handed back to the other students heavily redacted copies of their work often covered with red ink admonitions, "You cann't say that in English!" or "Use a dictsionery next time!" His classmates' ire was further enflamed when he would refer to himself in the third person as *Il Signore* Lanza, an act that totally flummoxed Dorothy Chen and almost caused the poor woman to flee her first class meeting.

Perry hoped, deep in a place he was almost too ashamed to acknowledge to his writing teacher's conscience, that *Il Signore* would now administer the *coup de grace* to Ellie's stunningly inane effort.

"Ellie, *cara*," the barber began in his heavily accented English. "I think you got seeds of a marvelous story here. Same like Dorothy, I enjoy many parts. 'Specially, when Miranda and Carlos drop water balloons off Getty Museum. But, same like Dorothy," he said, acknowledging the older woman (who shivered and turned away), "*Il Signore* gots a few problems. I mean. I no understanding when Miranda talk to her dog, JoJo. And she always asking him, 'JoJo, what *we* think?' Why she do that? Why she use first person plurals when talk to her dog? And then when Carlos have sex with the two *ermafrodite* he meets when he and Miranda are at Santa Anita race track, *Il Signore* absolute no get that."

"Now that you mention it," chimed in Bill Dworsky, "I didn't get *that* part either. I don' even know what a hermaphrodite is. I figured it's some kind of sacred virgin."

"Oh, for *God* sakes," said Patti Ditmar, her voice dripping with impatience. "Would someone *please* explain to our mechanic friend here what a hermaphrodite is. I mean, *really!*" She turned to him in a huff. "For crying out loud, Bill. It's a symbolic reference to Carlos' super masculinity and his ascendancy over Miranda." She turned to the author. "Isn't that right, Ellie?"

Ellie Jarvis looked around the room and smiled weakly. "I guess you'll just have to wait 'til next week to find out," she said, reaching into her backpack and producing six sets of manuscripts. "Here's the sequel. Only eighteen pages this time."

Perry Colangelo stared at *Miranda: Love Me or Don't* for several seconds before he reached out and took his copy, forcing himself to smile. "That's great. Just great. Thanks, Ellie." He looked around at his students, then suddenly smacked himself in the forehead. "Listen, folks. I'm *so* sorry but I totally forgot to mention that my mom in LA is getting married. I'm flying out tomorrow and won't be back for ten days. But you guys go ahead and meet next week without me . . . " The writing teacher's voice trailed off when he caught Dorothy Chen staring at him with a withering look of undisguised loathing.

#

In the Hallway

BEFORE RETIRING TO her own bedroom, Janet la Rossa kissed her husband of twenty-eight years on the mouth . . . for the second time that day!

Stunned into a surprised silence, Frederick la Rossa was left standing alone in the narrow upstairs hallway. *What the hell's going on?* he wondered. *What does it mean, these two kisses, this sudden show of affection?*

He had just emerged from the bathroom that had long served as a clear dividing line between their two bedrooms, between their two lives. He was cleanly shaven, freshly showered, teeth brushed, breath sweet. He had on his normal sleeping garb— light sweat pants and his favorite *'Viva Che'* tee shirt.

Jan had arrived at the top of the stairs carrying a book in her left hand, using her forefinger as a place mark. She was wearing a loosely tied white terry cloth bathrobe. Frederick la Rossa stepped aside to allow his wife a clear path to her own door. But Jan stopped in front of her husband. He backed up against the wall, giving her even more room to pass. His wife did not pass, however. Instead, she reached up her right hand, gently stroked his neck and left ear, looked fleetingly into his eyes, closed her own, and standing on tip toe, planted a short, soft kiss directly and firmly on his lips. Then she eased around him and walked the several paces to her bedroom. She entered quickly, without a backward glance, without a word, and closed the door.

Frederick la Rossa remained rooted, barefoot in mid-hallway, pondering this sudden change in his wife's demeanor.

The couple had long ago arrived at a mutually agreed upon arrangement: no casual touching. No kissing. Few loving words. Kind words, certainly—but delivered civilly, rather than affectionately. And certainly no sex, at least recently.

The last time they had coupled was four years earlier, during a furtive, State Department-be-damned week in Cuba. And the last time they embraced was three months ago—a hug at the airport, when Jan flew to Maryland to be with Ed, her dying father.

Frederick la Rossa recalled every detail of that last embrace.

Delivered to La Guardia, Jan was wearing a burgundy-colored long sleeved blouse that he bought her in Havana. She'd not bothered to change out of the faded jeans and tennis shoes she had on when she got the phone call with the news of her father. She'd stuffed her hair into a forest green bandana that didn't quite keep stubborn tufts of her riotous red hair from poking through. Standing next to her on the airport's sidewalk, he thought his wife looked gorgeous.

"Don't come in," she said hurriedly in her husky voice. "You don't need to wait in line with me. I'll be all right." She leaned toward him and they embraced. He was prepared for a not-overly-long hug. But Jan held on longer than he thought she would, her arms wrapped tightly around him. Finally, she pulled away and made a quick grab for her carry-on. "Not to worry," she said. "I'll call as soon as I get there. Be back home again before you know it." She hurried toward the automated doors, glancing back at him briefly, before disappearing into the terminal.

But Jan was *not* home before he knew it. Ed proved more resilient than the doctors had predicted. He lingered for three months while wife Beatrice and daughter Jan provided an alternating and dutiful vigil. 'Dutiful,' because in almost fifty years as spouse and father, Ed had rarely—and then only grudgingly—bestowed any sweetness or love or generosity upon either his wife or his only child. His imminent departure, therefore, was not seen as the tragic event it might have been. And neither woman was hypocrite enough to pretend that they would carry their grief terribly long.

While his wife was gone, Frederick had a lot of time to himself. He watched *The Motorcycle Diaries* twice and listened nightly to Tito Puente's music. From deep storage, he retrieved photo albums of their vacations: to Greece for their honeymoon; several trips to Italy; twice to New Zealand to visit friends; a dozen others to all points of the globe; and the last one, to Cuba, four years earlier.

One evening, half way through her absence, he retrieved a poem he had written to her when they were on the beach in Santiago de Cuba. He meant for Jan to see it then. But he chose not to show it to her, and when they returned home, he entered it into his computer where it remained hidden. Now, with Jan away, he printed it out and read it aloud while he stood in front of the fireplace.

"Good morning" is now unspoken.
A symbol of the token our affection has become.
Some promises were broken,
Others, better left undone.

Our life together – sullied,
our conversations sowed discord,
and neither partner worried
who came when, or who got bored.

We surprised our friends.
But it was no surprise to us.
They mourn for some lost paradise.
We just got off the bus.

A burning log spat an ember onto the stone hearth in front of him. He watched it as it smoldered red for longer than he supposed it should have.

In Baltimore, Ed hung on. He had better days and worse days. But at the end, he went quickly, quietly, and was buried. Jan stayed on for a few more days until Beatrice shooed her daughter home, assuring her that all would be well.

His wife's return this afternoon was as surprising in its way as her long-hug departure had been.

Again at La Guardia, at a pre-arranged spot they always used for pick-ups. Frederick la Rossa arrived early and leaned against a cement column, barely heated by the late afternoon sun. Winter was only reluctantly loosening its grip and he longed to be warm again. He sensed, more than heard, his wife's approach. When he opened his eyes, there she was, standing directly in front of him, dressed again—astonishingly—in burgundy and green. Jan pressed close to him. Quickly and unselfconsciously she gave her husband a hasty kiss on the lips. More like a single stroke of a very dry, very shy paintbrush. But a kiss on the lips, nonetheless.

During the drive home, Jan seemed only slightly misty, somewhat relieved, even strangely buoyant. "Mom's going to come and stay for a while, as soon she can. Will that be OK?"

"Absolutely," he answered quickly. He adored his mother-in-law.

They spoke of their three grown children. All well. All healthy. They would be filtering in over the next several weeks from school, from work.

Conversation that evening surrounded a light dinner and most of a bottle of Pinot Grigio. Jan said she was not yet ready to rehash the past months and felt she didn't really need to—they had spoken and emailed each other often during her father's illness. She insisted that he fill her in on his time alone. Frederick kept it short and factual. He talked about work, videos, music. He didn't mention the poem. Just past ten, he ended his summary.

"That's it for me," he said.

"Me too," she answered, then added, "I think I'll read for a bit."

Forty minutes later, with Jan now in her bedroom, Frederick la Rossa was alone in the upstairs hallway, having been kissed—unprecedentedly—twice today *on the lips*. His gaze wandered. At the end of the corridor there was an ice-frosted window that gave out onto their yard.

Unsteadily, he placed bare foot after bare foot on the hallway-length runner that covered the oak floor. He creaked his way to the window and looked out. *You wouldn't know it was spring,* he thought. A few patches of snow still stubbornly dotted the lawn. The pale glow of the street lamp across the road cast an iridescent, yellow sheen on the icy cobblestones where they met the curb. A cool breeze rattled the bare limbs of the birch trees in the yard.

He stood at the window for several minutes, taking in the night. Then he turned and walked back along the hallway. He passed his bedroom door, then the bathroom, and came to a halt outside his wife's room. There was no sound from within. The only sound Frederick la Rossa could hear was the wind in the birch branches, and the squeaking of the floorboards as he shifted his weight from foot to foot.

#

Crime on the Alaska / Russia border

by Richie Goldstein

Praise for
TRAFFIC NORTH

"An excellent mystery with wonderful, richly defined, unforgettable characters. As a resident of the lower 48, I also learned a great deal about Alaska, Russia and the seamier side of both cultures. The author is an excellent educator as well as a talented novelist!" —*Paul Canter*

"Richie Goldstein falls in love with every character. This is reading by a sweet waterfall, a gorgeous sunrise, with nothing but his words surrounding you. I love his writing. You will too." —*Marge Ford*

"A great read, especially all the well researched background and flavor of Alaska. I hope to read sequels!"
—*Betsy Rothstein*